I0581742

BITTEN BY THE NORTH WIND

BOOKS BY D. LIEBER

Minte and Magic

The Exiled Otherkin

The Assassin's Legacy

Intended Fates Trilogy

Intended Bondmates

Intended Strangers

Intended Enemies

Council of Covens

Dancing with Shades

In Search of a Witch's Soul

Also by D. Lieber

Conjuring Zephyr

Once in a Black Moon

A Very Witchy Yuletide

The Treason of Robyn Hood

The Curse of Moonseed Manor

The Goblin King's Mischief

The Winter Sorcerer and the Summer Witch

The Glass Moth

BITTEN BY THE NORTH WIND

D. LIEBER

First edition October 2025

Ink & Magick, LLC
Kenosha, Wisconsin
contact@inkandmagick.com

Special Edition ISBN: 978-1-951239-41-1
Hardcover ISBN: 978-1-951239-38-1
Paperback ISBN: 978-1-951239-39-8
Ebook ISBN: 978-1-951239-40-4

⚹ HUMAN AUTHORED

Reg #: 5606133, https://authorsguild.org/human

Cover by 100 Covers
Edited by Olivia Kalb at oliviakalbediting@gmail.com
Proofread by Samantha Talarico

To Óðinn.
For the gift of words, for the creative frenzy that birthed
this book,
I thank and honor you.

Thank you also to my beta readers John and Megan, and a very special hail! to Nina for all her help with my Heathenry and Norse mythology research.

ONE

"I fucking hate you," Thea croaked, her throat raw and her voice shaking as she stared at the man on the other side of the bars from her.

His green eyes softened, which pissed her off even more. But she didn't have the energy to muster more than a glare.

Pushing herself to a sitting position on the cold basement floor, she groaned. Her muscles were sore, and her bones were still loose from shifting back to human form. Her clothes, which had stayed on during her transformation, were misshapen, and she moved her shoulders so her shirt would sit right.

"I'll run you a bath," Syver said, standing from his crouch to unlock the door of the cage where she'd spent the night.

Thea wanted to tell him not to bother, wanted to tell him that she would shower when she got home. But she knew that probably wasn't a good idea. She surveyed the floor of the cage. There were goosefeathers everywhere—remnants of the high-end dog bed Syver had put in there for her. If she looked half as disheveled as the space did, her neighbors might call the cops just from worry.

It didn't matter anyway. She hadn't been home for more than a few minutes over the past few months, just long enough to grab the things she needed. And he'd accompanied her, so it wasn't as if she'd been able to enjoy her own space.

Shuffling toward the open cage door, Thea wondered how her life had come to this. She had a good job—nothing glamorous, but a cozy office job that paid her bills. She'd been up for a pay raise within the next year. She'd paid off her car. She even had a good relationship with her parents. Her life had been quiet and comfortable. She'd been the type to stay in and eat pizza while watching an old movie rather than go out and party hard on the weekends.

She'd never thought that accepting the offer of a coffee date from the handsome guy who worked down the hall would lead to all this.

As she made her way through the dimly lit basement to the stairs, she remembered thinking how lucky she was. All the single women in the office— even some of the married ones—had a crush on Syver. Half of them flushed whenever he was in the room. He was otherworldly, the kind of hot she almost couldn't think around, tall and sculpted as if he spent every moment of his free time working out. His dark hair was short but still long enough to grab a hold of in her unprofessional fantasies. And those green eyes? She'd felt like she couldn't even move when he looked at her. It was primal instinct—as if any motion would encourage him to give chase.

How lucky, right? She'd been so fucking lucky when he'd asked her out. She'd walked on air. She'd worn her favorite heels and her lucky earrings.

Little had she known…

Now, she could barely look at him without rage filling her gut. Then again, rage was almost all she felt these days.

He said it would get better, and if she was being honest, it had. But she still wasn't back to normal.

She could hear the water running in the bathroom before she even reached the landing.

Syver waited for her outside the bathroom door. "I put a fresh towel in there for you. Do you need any help?"

Thea growled and bared her teeth at him. "You fucking wish."

Even two months ago, she'd needed help getting undressed and moving around the day after the full moon, so this was progress, indeed.

Syver snorted and smirked, all the sympathy he'd shown her not ten minutes before gone. "Not as much as you do."

Her face flushed at the reminder that she'd once welcomed his hands on her. She clenched her jaw so she wouldn't take a bite out of him, then slipped into the bathroom without another word, wishing she knew how to hurt him as much as he'd hurt her.

Staring at her reflection in the mirror, she was relieved to see she didn't look nearly as bad as last time. Her golden brown hair was a rat's nest of goosefeathers, and her brown eyes were a little more amber than usual. With dark circles under them, they looked tired. But once she was cleaned up, it would look more like she'd stayed up all night reading a good book than she'd turned into a wolf and tried to tear apart anything and everything she got her claws into.

She frowned as she pulled off her shirt, noting she still hadn't gained back the weight she'd lost. She'd always been happy with her soft, gentle curves and hadn't gotten used to the hardness of a werewolf's body. Her favorite clothes didn't fit, and she hadn't been stable enough to go out into a crowded place to buy new ones.

Of course, with all the time she was taking off work, she probably shouldn't spend money anyway. If it wasn't for telework, she'd be broke.

She untied the drawstring that kept her too-big pants up and finished undressing before slipping into the hot water of the bath.

As she sank into weightlessness, her tired muscles relaxed, and she let out a heavy breath.

In the other room, she could hear Syver going about making breakfast and smell the delicious scent of white sausages. Her favorite.

She frowned, annoyed that he knew and catered to what she liked best.

I wonder if I've come far enough that it's safe for me

to go out in public. I'm going to ask him. No, I'm going to tell him. I can't stay locked up in this house forever. I need to get out, get back to the office, buy some new clothes at least. I have an entire month until the next full moon. I should be fine.

to go out in public. I'm going to ask him. No, I'm going to tell him. I can't stay locked up in this house forever. I need to get out, get back to the office, buy some new clothes at least. I have an entire month until the next full moon. I should be fine.

TWO

Syver frowned. Thea's request focused the emotions swirling inside him—pity, guilt, desire—the feelings he still hadn't managed to master in her presence. He knew this day would come sooner or later.

"You want to go into town?" he asked slowly before scooping scrambled eggs into his mouth.

"I'm going into town," she corrected, her amber eyes challenging him to disagree. "It's starting to get cold now, and none of my clothes fit."

He perked up at the sound of her voice and the look in her eyes. This fierceness in Thea's personality had only surfaced after she'd been turned. At the very least, she'd never shown this side of herself to him before then. He smirked and enjoyed how his expression earned him a look of irritation from her. And though this intensity from her only stoked the fire within him, he tamped down on the compulsion to pursue where that road led. The itch under his skin grew worse every time he had to resist, but she wouldn't welcome his touch.

Her hair was still wet from the bath, and he could smell her freshly scrubbed skin and the scent of his shampoo in her hair. Her pointed chin was lifted and her perfect mouth set.

Pushing away his awakened arousal as he'd been doing so often over the last five months, Syver considered her words. *She has been doing better.*

"All right." He nodded. "I'll take you to a thrift store out in the county. There shouldn't be too many people on a weekday."

She shook her head. "No, I'm going by myself. I've been with you practically twenty-four seven for five months. I need some time to myself."

Syver rubbed his palm against his stubbly facial hair. "Okay. I'll drop you off at your car and pick you up later." *And I will follow you every step of the way.*

Syver had seen Thea's progress over the last couple of months. With the full moon over, the worst of the danger was behind them for a while. He knew she would need to gain confidence to stand on her own, but that didn't mean he wouldn't be there to protect her and anyone she might maul should she lose control.

Thea's expression brightened as she smiled at him for the first time in months. His chest warmed. *Maybe there's hope for me yet.*

"It'll be a relief not to have to look at you for a few hours," she said.

Or not…

He flashed a sardonic smile. "I know my beauty can be exhausting to look upon."

Her face flushed, and she squinted at him, clearly annoyed. His smile turned genuine. If nothing else, she still found him attractive. He knew that. And he would use any advantage he could to wiggle his way into her heart. He was shameless in that way.

Swallowing her last bite of breakfast, Thea stood from the table.

"Since I readily agreed to your outing, I'd like something in return," Syver announced.

Thea froze. "And what's that?" she asked with hesitation.

"Next full moon, I want you to come on a trip with me."

She bit her lip. Whether she was worried about going somewhere unknown with him or her own control over her other side, he wasn't sure. "Where?"

"Next month is Winter Nights. It's time for you to make your first blót to Hati."

How many times had Syver tried to explain the more nuanced aspects of being a mánagarmr to Thea over the last five months? She needed to know where they came from and their traditions. With Thea appearing more comfortable with testing her limits, perhaps she was calm enough to listen to something more than the basics of how to survive. Perhaps she was ready to open herself to the broader possibilities of what this new life could offer her. At the very least, she was asking him for a favor, and that opened her to a quid pro quo.

"What does that mean?" she questioned, sitting back down in the chair across from him.

Pushing his empty plate away, Syver rested his elbows on the table and laced his fingers. He forced his expression to be neutral, not wanting to show his pleasure at the opportunity to have a civil conversation with her or the possibility that she was finally ready to listen to what this life could offer her. "The short version is: Hati is the father of all werewolves. Three times a year, werewolves gather and offer him sacrifice. Your first blót is particularly important. It's when you accept your new identity as a child of Hati. In return, he should bless you with more control and clarity."

"Should?"

Syver shrugged a little, spreading his palms. "It depends on whether you truly accept this new part of yourself or not. If you come to him with false words, he also has the power to make it much worse."

Thea shuddered, then took up her plate again. "I make no promises… I'll think about it."

Syver nodded once. *I guess that's good enough for now.*

It hadn't taken him this long to get used to being a werewolf, but then, he'd been much younger than her, still a child. At the time, he'd just been happy to finally have a family of sorts, a place where he belonged.

He rose from the table and took his plate to the sink. "I'll just check my email before we go," he said as she poured herself more coffee.

He'd been working from home a lot over the last

few months in order to keep an eye on her, but he'd been taking three days off every month—the full moon and the days before and after—to help her through. If he checked his email now, he wouldn't have any surprises tomorrow.

CHAPTER

THREE

Thea adjusted her shoulders against the uncomfortable feeling of Syver standing behind her. Though he wasn't close enough for her to feel his body heat, the solidity of his presence was hard to ignore. She hated how her stomach still fluttered when he was close to her. "Leave already," she demanded as she slid her key into her apartment door.

The wind had a cold bite to it despite the late summer warmth of the sun. She'd loved this apartment the moment she'd seen it. It was set up in a motel rather than a hotel style. The front door led directly to the parking lot, and the back sliding glass door opened onto a patio that faced a small lake. It was a small complex, too—no more than ten units.

"Call me when you're ready for me to pick you up," Syver insisted.

Thea snorted. "I'm never going to be ready for that."

She knew there was no way Syver would let her out of his sight. He'd given in way too easily. But she would pretend along with him just for some space.

Once inside, she slammed the door in his face, hoping she wouldn't see him again for a few hours. Then she took a deep breath, closing her eyes in a moment of true solitude. But she frowned when she opened them again. Her lovely apartment, her little safe haven, looked foreign to her. It was just as she'd left it, but for a little more dust. Her blue couch looked just as cozy as ever with her favorite sherpa throw blanket over one arm. Her scented candles were lined up neatly on her coffee table.

As she moved toward the kitchen, she saw that her collection of mugs still hung on the hooks near her electric kettle. So why didn't this place feel as familiar as it had before?

She clicked her tongue as her gaze alighted on the devil's ivy plant that twisted and twirled around her kitchen. The leaves were yellowed, and some had fallen off. She'd had it since college. Rushing to the sink, as if the extra seconds would save the thing, she filled her kettle with water and hoped it could be revived.

As the excess water poured from the hole at the bottom of the hanging pot, it hit the metal bucket beneath it. She winced against the sound, so loud in her ears, like a thunderstorm on a tin roof.

Her too-sensitive hearing triggered her other side, and she felt the now-familiar heat rush through her blood. For once, she didn't panic. She took a deep breath in through her nose, concentrating on the cool air in her nostrils and the expansion of her chest. She was fine. That sound was not dangerous. There was no need to wolf out over something like that.

She wouldn't have been able to stand the shame of returning to Syver's with no clothes because she'd stumbled at the tiniest of hurdles.

Straightening her spine, she went to the hall closet to grab her winter coat and hat. She wasn't sure when she would be able to come back, and those were not things she needed to buy just because she'd lost a little weight.

Folding her coat over her arm, she exited the front door, smiling to see Syver nowhere in sight.

Her mood lifted immediately, and for the first time in a while, she thought she might actually have a good day.

As she twisted her key in the lock, the sound of a neighbor's door opening pricked her ears. Taking another deep breath through her nose, she caught an unfamiliar scent like vanilla cappuccino and warm amber. She glanced over to see someone she'd never met.

She tilted her head at the man who stepped out from where the nosy widow Mrs. White lived, a small trash bag in one hand. He didn't appear particularly tall, perhaps a few inches taller than her, but his build seemed like someone who used his body to earn a living. His dark blond hair was only long enough to look untamable, and his blue-green eyes had a lost sort of quality to them—as if he'd misplaced something. She didn't recognize him at all.

He smiled self-consciously at her and raised a half-hearted hand in greeting. "Hello."

With a polite smile, Thea returned his sentiment.

"I'm the new neighbor," he added awkwardly.

Ah, so not a relative of Mrs. White's, then. She must've moved out.

"I just moved here from Chicago. I've met most everyone in the building—a friendly bunch. I thought the unit next door was empty."

Is he the over-explaining type? Thea watched the man shift his weight from one foot to the other. *Cute.*

"I've just been busy lately, so I'm not here much," she said with a friendly smile. "Chicago, huh? This must be quite the change for you."

He nodded, encouraged and clearly relieved she hadn't brushed him off or ignored him. "It is. I didn't even know my neighbors in Chicago, let alone the whole building. And I'm still getting used to the area. I don't even know a good burger joint yet."

"Oh, if you're looking for a good burger, you're going to want to go to The Stop. They also have the best onion rings you'll ever eat."

Her new neighbor grinned. "Thanks for the recommendation. I'll have to check it out. Oh, I'm Eero, by the way."

Eero moved to close the distance between them, offering his hand.

She chuckled at him, his rush akin to holding the door open for someone still fifteen feet away.

"Thea," she said, placing her hand in his.

"It's nice to meet you, Thea." His tone was softer and warmer now that he was so close.

"You, too."

Releasing her, he met her eyes before averting his gaze. "Listen, I was just wondering, and don't feel pressured in any way, but I haven't met many people my age yet. So, if you're up for it, again totally fine if you're not, but when you're free, how about we go for that burger together?"

Though his face was directed at his feet, he glanced up at her hopefully.

She smiled. She already liked this unobtrusive man. He was so much the opposite of Syver and his overly masculine confidence that she found Eero endearing.

"Sure, all right. I'll tell you all the best things to do and see in the area, too."

Eero's eyes widened in slight surprise as if he'd expected her to decline. He reached into his shorts pocket and pulled out his phone.

"Great," he sighed happily. "Let me get your number so we can coordinate times. You said you've been busy, so I don't want to inconvenience you."

Thea told him her number, and he immediately sent her a text so she had his.

Dipping his head, Eero backed up slowly. "Well, I better"—he held up the small trash bag in his hand—"you know, finish taking the trash out. I'll, uh, I'll text you."

Thea couldn't help but giggle. "Okay. See ya."

FOUR

"Hati, hound birthed in Ironwood, give me strength. As you know you will someday swallow Máni, lend me your patience in this moment." Syver gripped the steering wheel as he muttered a prayer between his clenched jaws.

From this distance, he couldn't hear what the man with the trash bag was saying to Thea, but his body language was clear enough.

Syver told himself Thea didn't belong to him, especially now that she could hardly stand the sight of him. But those rational words meant little to the wolf inside him.

His hands trembled as his knuckles whitened, and he could feel his vision sharpen and his blood howl. How dare this upstart human approach her?

His breath was coming in short bursts, no presence of mind to control it.

Syver watched as Thea smiled and waved at the man, her eyes warm while she tucked her hair behind her ear. She'd never looked at him like that before, never shown him that expression.

Somewhere in his rational mind, he knew she'd shown him other things, more intimate, vulnerable things, but that part of his brain was too quiet at the moment. Too loud was the desire to close his jaws around the man's throat.

Syver's gaze followed Thea as she climbed into her car, his breath coming easier with every step she took away from her neighbor.

Syver shook his head at himself, releasing a steadying sigh. As she pulled out of the parking lot, he followed after her.

Maybe I should send her to Rorik.

Rorik was the mánagarmr who'd turned him when he was just a skittish young boy. Rorik had taught Syver everything there was to know about being a mánagarmr, and Syver had full confidence Rorik could teach Thea as well.

A thought that had been forming in the back of Syver's mind finally solidified. Thea had too much power over him, too much influence—not that she knew it. Seeing how he'd just reacted to her talking to a strange man, it was clear the last few months of isolation had been just as much for him as it had been for her. When had she gained such a foothold in his life? When he'd turned her?

She's come so far that she's testing her ability to venture out alone. What will happen when I'm not following her? How will I handle her being out of my sight?

His stomach twisted, and his mind jumped away

from the thought as if it had burned him. He bit his lip, recognizing that this reaction in him was troubling.

"I'll call Rorik," he said to himself in the empty car. "I'll ask him if he knows anything about this attachment. Maybe it's entirely normal when you've newly turned someone. And I'll ask him if…" He trailed off the rest of his statement. He couldn't even say aloud that he would ask Rorik to take Thea in and teach her. The thought was too much to speak into being.

As he'd suggested, Thea headed toward the thrift store out in the county rather than the crowded outlet mall. As much as she fought him every step of the way, she did listen to his advice. She defied him more in spirit than in action. Hers was a kind heart, and he knew she didn't want to hurt anyone.

She'd been devastated that first full moon. He would never forget the look on her face when she'd awoken smeared with blood. He pushed the memory from his mind. She'd come a long way since then.

There were only two other cars in the parking lot. Syver parked his car around the back, out of sight should she leave before he could move. After a few minutes, enough time for her to get to the back where they kept the clothes, he slipped into the shop.

The shop was part thrift store, part antique mall, with many tall shelves he could easily hide behind to keep an eye on her.

Syver quickly assessed the situation. There was an older man behind the counter who didn't bother to look up at his entrance. There was also a short woman, a young child in tow, inspecting a collection of glassware near the automatic doors.

Syver immediately zoned in on Thea's scent. He could hear the soft sound of her sneakers on the waxed floor and the rustle of her clothes as her arms swung with the rhythm of her walk. Lurking in her direction, he listened carefully to her easy breathing, steady and calm.

Could she distinguish his scent from the others? Had she progressed so far? Could she hear his careful footfalls?

By all rights, they should have come together for her first outing. He should have been able to ask her those questions, coached her awareness from the front line. That's how it should've been. That was how it had been for him and Rorik.

This is fine. He tried to soothe his disappointment. *She's doing well enough that she probably won't need me for much longer.*

He didn't want to think about what would happen then. He already knew that when he declared her fully ready for the world, when he had taught her everything she needed to know to survive as a mánagarmr, she would leave. If he ever saw her again, it would be at work.

No, I still have time to win her over. Her temper may cool the more she gets used to this new life when she sees what it has to offer her.

Syver listened uneasily to the slight squeaking of hangers as Thea looked through the shop's clothing selection. He wondered if he was more nervous than she was. From what he could hear and smell, she seemed relaxed and comfortable.

His tense muscles, ready to step in should she need him, eased as his dread increased. He needed more time if he was going to convince her to stay.

While Syver stewed in his own malaise, the front door opened as a new customer entered. Syver marked the woman's progress through the shop. She moved easily with a loose, comfortable gait toward where Thea was.

This will be a good test for her.

The strong scent of weed wafted into his nose like a skunk sauntering down the aisle. He snuffled, shaking his head as if he could shake the scent out. And then he realized he couldn't hear Thea.

FIVE

Thea froze as the woman neared her. The smell of pot was pungent, strong in an inescapable way. She held her breath for a moment to assess how she felt.

She'd steeled herself before coming into the store, pushed all outside sensory stimuli to the background like Syver had taught her. The whining of the child who was bored and impatient to leave didn't bother her. The smell of old books, rust, and dust were fine.

She took a tentative breath through her mouth so as not to overwhelm her nose.

But before she could even feel pleased that she was firmly in her human form, bothered by the scent of skunk no more than a human would be, she found herself pinned against the clothes rack.

Shirts scattered to the floor, and the hangers still on the rod dug painfully into her back as Syver's hard body pressed against her.

Thea flushed. Desire pooled within her. How long

had it been since he'd held her, since he'd touched her? *Too long.*

She clenched her jaw. After everything, she was disgusted with herself for reacting to him in that way.

"What the—?" Thea's rage built inside her, overshadowing the craving he'd elicited.

"Hey!" the woman who'd just arrived snapped. "What do you think you're doing?" She stepped out from the other side of the clothes rack and planted her feet. "Let go of her. You can't come up and grab people like that."

Thea raised her eyebrows. The woman was taller than average but skinny. She couldn't believe she'd challenge a man as large and intimidating as Syver.

"Mind your business," Syver growled near Thea's ear. She couldn't see his face, but she could feel his tension.

"Oh, you made it my business by assaulting her in public," the woman shot back.

Clearly done discussing the matter, Syver grabbed Thea around the waist and lifted her off the floor to carry her away.

Thea wiggled from his grasp. "Let go." She pushed his hands away from her. "For fuck's sake, I'm fine."

The woman inched toward her in a protective stance.

Thea glanced at her and held up a hand in a calming gesture. "It's fine. I know him."

Pursing her lips, the woman squinted at the hulking werewolf before her. "Are you sure?" she asked in a hushed voice.

Thea nodded. "Thanks. Really, it's fine." Then she

snapped her head around to glare at Syver. "God damn it. You ruin everything. I'll just buy them online. *Fuck!*"

Turning on her heel, she stormed through the aisles toward the front door, aware that he was following her but refusing to look back at him.

After climbing into her car, she leaned her forehead on the steering wheel—her rage giving way to embarrassment. *What is wrong with him? I was fine…unless he saw something I didn't?*

She replayed the scene in her mind. Even after he'd pounced on her, even when she was royally pissed, she'd still been in control. She hadn't felt her teeth or fingernails elongate. She hadn't felt that tell-tale itch of unnatural hair growth. She certainly hadn't felt the molten heat in her bones as they prepared to change shape.

Of course, she'd been nothing but pissed since he'd explained what he'd done to her. She was quite used to the feeling. Perhaps all the heightened emotions over the last five months had given her more practice than she'd thought.

Sighing heavily, she leaned back in her seat. Her eyes met Syver's through the windshield. He stood unnaturally still, watching her from just outside the front entrance.

Thea clicked her tongue and curled her lip. Then she flipped him off. The gesture wasn't nearly as satisfying or cathartic as she'd thought it would be.

Turning on the ignition with more force than necessary, she revved the engine, then peeled out of the parking lot.

Once she was on the road, she pushed all her feelings aside. She wanted him to see her anger more than she wanted to feel it. She'd have more than enough time later to brood over what had happened. He'd followed her when he'd said she could go alone. Even though she knew he would all along, he hadn't kept up his end of the farce. He'd jumped the gun. He hadn't trusted she was in control. She couldn't be more embarrassed that he'd caused a scene in public. But, deep down, she knew that what bothered her most was her body's reaction to his touch, to his proximity, even to the idea that he would jump in to protect her from accidentally hurting someone. She couldn't deal with that feeling right now. She needed to be mad. She needed her rage to get her through this period of adjustment so she could get away from him.

Her rage was what helped her think straight. Her rage kept her from turning back into the giddy fool she'd been whenever he was around. She made too many idiotic decisions related to him when she wasn't angry. The soft rumble of his stupid voice, the stupid glint in his eyes while he was trying not to laugh, and especially that stupid fucking confident smile like he knew the effect he had on her.

It was all annoying, and all the more because she couldn't stop herself from finding it attractive somehow. Where was her pride? Where was her feminist spirit? Was she so shallow as to fall for a pretty face?

As thoughts of how he'd helped her surfaced in her mind—how he'd hid what she'd done that first full moon, how he'd trained her to control and understand her other side, how he hadn't abandoned her as he could have—even as she saw clearly the fleeting moments of pity and sorrow in his eyes, heard the apology she'd refused to acknowledge, she smothered it. She snuffed out all those thoughts and feelings like a flame deprived of air.

She needed her rage. It was the only way she could leave. The only way she would ever stand on her own again.

SIX

S yver removed his seatbelt and leaned back in his seat with a heavy sigh. The midday sun shined off the rear window of Thea's car in his driveway. The woods around his house were hushed but for the squirrels industriously going about their nut gathering in preparation for winter.

Everything was fine now. She was safely back in his house.

He hated to admit it, but he was starting to think he was the problem. He had seemed to have far less control over his inner wolf than she had during the exchange at the thrift store. And once his body had been pressed against hers, he couldn't think of anything else. It took everything in him not to plow right through that woman who'd stood between him and carrying Thea out of there.

Then again, when had he ever had control over himself when it came to Thea? He was fooling himself if he ever believed it to be true. It was his inability to control himself around her that had brought all of this about.

He'd lost control. Her touch had so riled him that he'd slipped just a little. And his kiss had turned into the scrape of an elongated tooth.

With her warmth and his own shame still fresh in his mind, he couldn't help but think of the night that had gotten them into all of this, the night he'd turned her.

Thea smiled, the starlight shining in her brown eyes as she looked up at the sky.

Syver sat beside her—their feet in the cold water —on a short dock on the lake at the back of her apartment.

The gentle sound of the rippling water was calming in the hushed night.

He took in the sight of her gazing upward, not bothering to hide his blatant stare.

Syver didn't think he'd ever met anyone as sweet as her. She was shy and gentle in a way that drew him in. He didn't regret ignoring his rule about not dating women from work in the least. He wanted to know more. What other facets of her personality would she show him the more comfortable she got? Already, two dates in, she was more capable of carrying on a conversation with him than before he'd asked her out for coffee.

At dinner, they'd talked about work and the movies they liked. The way her smile lit her face with pure joy warmed his heart as well as other parts of him.

He thought it would be a relief to get her alone, away from the prying eyes of the other people at the restaurant. But the moment the gentle night enveloped them, he became unbearably aware of her every move. Every lick of her lips, every flutter of her eyelashes, every soft giggle, he saw it all with tense attention—with the attention of a wolf watching a rabbit.

She must have felt his eyes on her because she glanced over to meet his gaze. Even in the dim light, he could see her cheeks flush.

"Thank you for inviting me out again," she said in a hushed tone.

He frowned at the slight inflection in her voice—the little emphasis on the first word that said their night together was almost over.

"I'm glad you enjoyed it," he said low, leveling a purposeful gaze at her.

Her breath caught, and her eyelashes fluttered. A satisfied smile spread across his face as he leaned toward her. She tilted her chin up, accepting his approach.

Her lips were soft and plump. They tasted like the strawberry wine she'd had at dinner and mango lip balm. She trembled when he leaned closer, deepening their kiss.

His blood heated, and his cock stiffened.

Syver pulled back to gauge Thea's reaction. Her lips parted with desire, and he could smell the slick heat pooling between her legs.

He smirked. "I'd like to stay…if you don't mind."

She bit her lip as if she couldn't wait to see what he would do next, then nodded slightly.

He turned toward her more fully, kissing her again. Water splashed as she removed her feet from the lake to better face him.

She moaned softly when he slipped the tip of his tongue into her mouth. The sound triggered something inside him, and an urgency he'd never experienced raced through him.

Seizing her waist, he pulled her on top of him so that her thighs straddled his hips. The skirt of her short blue dress slipped up her thighs, the fabric sleek as he ran his hands over it.

She pulled back, glancing around them quickly. All was quiet. The only lights were from the apartment building—their brilliance not reaching them—all but one were soft glows behind curtains.

She flashed him a mischievous smile, and all rational thought left his mind.

Lifting herself on her knees, she reached between her legs, fumbling for the zipper on his pants. As she quickly undid them, she whispered, "I'm on birth control."

Freeing his cock, she met his gaze. She must have seen his consent in his expression because she pulled her panties to one side and slowly lowered herself onto him.

He shuddered and gripped her backside, a bestial moan escaping his lips. Yes, this was it, the culmination of their every interaction thus far, what he'd wanted since the moment he'd laid eyes on her. It all made sense now.

She shushed him softly. "We have to be quiet if you don't want to get caught." Her hushed voice quivered with pleasure.

The tether he had on his control, the leash that was always so taut when she was around, broke. The scent of her arousal, strawberry wine and mango lip balm, the sound of her breathing heavily in his ear, trying to smother her own moans, and the tight heat of her surrounding his manhood as he slid in and out of her. He couldn't handle it. His mind grew foggy and went to a place somehow both surreal and far away as well as sharp and keen, with every sense overwhelmed—not unlike how he felt during the full moon.

He held her to him, pressing kisses to her neck. He could feel the molten heat start in his jaw, but it was too far away. He was inside her. She clutched him to her, and that was all that mattered.

Thea appeared in the upstairs window for only a second before shutting the curtains, the movement drawing his mind back to the present. He had to admit to himself that it wasn't a one-off. It might have been an accident, but he should've recognized the effect she'd had on him—the effect she still had on him—before it was too late. One thing was for certain though: It was getting worse. Defeat hardened his stomach as he grabbed his phone and pulled up Rorik's number.

"I was starting to wonder when I'd hear from you," Rorik said, answering almost immediately. "You've never gone this long without calling before."

Syver remained silent. He couldn't bring himself to say it.

"Hello? Syver?"

Syver cleared his throat. "I…have something to tell you." Thankfully, his voice was steady at least.

"Okay…" Syver's controlled tone didn't seem to have an effect because Rorik's reply was tight and guarded.

"I turned someone."

Syver steeled himself to weather Rorik's displeasure. Since shortly after Syver had been turned, Rorik had impressed upon him never to turn anyone. He had no idea why, but he trusted Rorik wouldn't insist if it wasn't important.

"Have you made any oaths?" Rorik asked urgently.

Syver shook his head. "No."

Rorik sighed at the other end. "That's good at least," he mumbled. "Is this why you haven't been in touch?"

Syver blinked at Rorik's lack of wrath. He didn't even demand an explanation as to why or how he'd done the thing he'd always been told not to do.

"Yes, I thought it would be better if I could acclimate her a little first. It…it was an accident," he added lamely, still feeling like he needed to explain.

"It was inevitable," Rorik stated.

Syver tilted his head.

"How are things going with the newly turned? Is she getting used to it? It must have been quite the shock if she didn't choose this for herself. Any problems?"

Syver frowned. "Yeah, there's a problem, but I think it's with me."

"What do you mean?"

"Thea is doing fine overall. She's still angry about the whole thing, so the transformation is more painful than it needs to be. She fights it too much. But she's in control. She still seems surprised sometimes by her heightened senses and emotions, but she doesn't let them trigger the shift… When you turn someone, are you supposed to feel…affected by them?"

"Affected how?" Rorik asked curiously.

Syver groaned. "I don't know how to describe it. It's like I want to give her everything she asks for. Even things she doesn't ask for, I'm trying to guess her every whim and desire. A man approached her today, and I nearly ripped his throat out. I thought she was in danger of shifting at the store, and I practically tackled her when she was just fine."

Rorik was silent for a while before answering. "I felt…protective of you when you first turned because you were still a child. Though you chose to stay with us, to become one of us, you were still quite young and had many things to learn as all children do. But have you considered that you just…like her?"

Rorik's words struck him like a note out of key.

"You know we're territorial by nature, protective if

we feel those we care about are threatened. As for the rest, wanting to give her everything she wants, that's a normal response when you're trying to win over someone you like. You said she's angry about the change. Is she angry at you?"

"She's beyond furious with me."

Rorik chuckled, and the sound made Syver feel twenty years younger. "There you have it. The woman you want is mad at you. Of course, you're trying anything you can to get into her good graces."

Rorik's explanation felt too simple, too easy, too mundane to encapsulate what he was feeling toward Thea. It wasn't as if he hadn't liked someone before. This was so over the top that he'd been sure it was werewolf related. But Rorik had been a mánagarmr for much longer than Syver, so he would know better.

"Are you bringing her with you to the Winter Nights blót?" Rorik interrupted Syver's thoughts.

"I'm hoping to, but I need to be sure she's ready to fully accept her new life."

Rorik hummed in agreement. "Well, let me know. The best advice I can give you is to be honest. You have the annoying habit of hiding behind bravado. Unless she knows you well, it might push her away."

Syver scowled. "It's not bravado."

"Oh? So you're just as much the blowhard ass you present yourself to be?"

"Who do you think I get it from?" Syver muttered.

Rorik barked a laugh. "Perhaps. But if you want something real, something true, with this woman, you're going to have to let her past all the strutting and preening."

Syver pursed his lips in distaste.

"Or don't. What do I know? I'm just an old bachelor who lost the woman I loved long ago."

Syver's heart squeezed. He'd seen Rorik's pain in fleeting, veiled moments. He'd caught him sneaking the old photo from his desk drawer on more than one occasion. But Rorik had truly loved that woman in the frame. Syver didn't…he didn't…love Thea, right?

A lump formed in Syver's throat, and he tried to swallow around it as his mouth went dry.

Would he be old and alone like Rorik one day? He'd never wanted for female companionship when the desire had struck him. Surely, he could find someone else to keep him company once Thea was gone.

He sucked in a breath as his stomach dropped.

"I'll think about what you said," Syver said softly, unable to put any convincing force behind his words.

He could hear the smile in Rorik's voice. "You do that." The smile disappeared. "And Syver? Do not make any oaths. Got it?"

"I won't." Syver repeated the same words he'd said most of his life.

"Good. I'll check back with you again about whether you're coming as the next full moon gets closer."

"All right. Talk to you later."

SEVEN

Thea was so angry that she couldn't form words to speak to Syver for the rest of the day. She didn't speak to him when he called her for meals, and she didn't say goodnight to him when she headed up to bed. She would normally at least have had a snide remark, but not this time.

Tomorrow, she would tell him she wanted to return home. After going over everything again and again, she felt she was ready to be in her own apartment when it wasn't the full moon at least.

This can't go on. After brushing her teeth and washing her face, she shuffled into the only bedroom, which Syver had vacated for her the last few months —when she wasn't spending the night in the cage downstairs that was.

As she settled between the cool sheets, her muscles relaxed. This was her favorite time of the day. She could hear the nighttime creatures rustling the newly fallen leaves in the woods outside the window.

She could even smell that it would rain overnight. All was peaceful and quiet. There was nothing she needed to do or say or be.

Closing her eyes, her ears picked out the gentle sounds of Syver settling onto the couch in the living room. If she listened hard enough, she could hear him breathing, she could hear the rustle of fabric as he removed his shirt and pulled the worn afghan over his broad shoulders.

She shivered under her blanket, knowing just how warm it would be to lie beside him. Squeezing her eyes tighter, she rolled onto her side and forced herself to sleep. But she would find no rest there as she relived a nightmare from the past.

Everything was too loud and too bright—the crickets, the wind, the glow from the overhead lights. She felt sticky and sore all over. She twitched a finger and hissed at the pain that shot up her arm, then hissed again at her own sound, which stabbed her eardrums.

She was tired, so very tired. Even fighting sleep seemed painful. She struggled to raise her eyelids.

"It's all right," Syver said softly, so softly that it didn't hurt her ears. "Don't worry. I'll take care of it."

Take care of what? What's he even doing here? As her mind fought to focus, she finally saw through her confusion to what he was talking about.

She was in her apartment, the sliding glass door wide open and the cool spring breeze blowing in. It was only just before dawn. The sky was lightening, but the sun had yet to crest the horizon.

Syver cradled her in his arms, rocking in a soothing motion while wiping her wet hair from her face. His hand was red with blood.

Then she smelled it—she tasted it—that unmistakable metallic taste. It was in her mouth, on her tongue.

His hand was stained because her face and hair were thick with the stuff.

As panic, confusion, and despair rose in her throat, her breathing became harsh and ragged.

"What's—what's happening to me?" her voice trembled in a half-sob. "What did I do?"

Syver's eyes shifted, only for a second, to something to her left. There, half on the patio and half on the carpet just inside the door, were two halves of a fawn—its beautiful brown eyes grotesque and horrible with the lack of life's light.

Thea choked on her own breath, shaking as her bones started to heat like molten lead.

She tried to scream in pain, but she couldn't get enough air for the sound to come out right.

"Look at me," Syver said, his voice firm and nonnegotiable.

Thea's eyes locked on his. *Have his eyes always been so green?* She remembered they were green before, but she couldn't recall the flecks of gold and copper. Why did they look so bright all of a sudden?

"Listen to the sound of my voice and only the sound of my voice."

His voice was soothing and steady, the caress of velvet on bare skin.

"Do you feel me?" He lifted his bloody hand to her face again, gently stroking her cheek with his thumb.

She nodded once.

"Concentrate on me. Think hard. What does it feel like?"

The heat in her bones subsided as she focused on his touch. "It's nice. I like it," she croaked.

"Take a slow breath, not too deep."

Thea took a shallow breath in through her nose.

"Now a little deeper."

She did as she was told until she felt normal in her own skin again.

"I know you have a lot of questions," Syver said. "I'll explain everything. But right now, we need to get you cleaned up."

Scooping her into his arms, he carried her to the bathroom, where he set her on the closed toilet before drawing her a bath.

Returning to her, he gently instructed, "Lift your arms."

Carefully, he peeled the sticky, stained clothes from her skin. She hadn't the presence of mind to be embarrassed. She was too tired, and it wasn't as if he hadn't seen it all anyways.

After helping her into the bath, he washed her hair and skin. She might have even enjoyed it but for the circumstances and her own exhaustion. She did giggle when he washed between her toes though.

He dried her with the fluffiest towel she owned,

then helped her into fresh pajamas. By the time he'd tucked her into bed, she couldn't even keep her eyes open.

"Sleep," he whispered. "I'll take care of everything."

By the time she woke late the next afternoon, it was like nothing had ever happened. The carpet, the patio, the bathtub, and even her clothes were spotless. It was the smell of chicken noodle soup simmering on the stove in the kitchen that had awoken her. It was as if it had all been a dream. And she might have believed it had been were it not for the serious expression on Syver's face when she shuffled into the dining room.

His green eyes were solemn, and his mouth was set. "I'm sorry" were the first words from his lips.

CHAPTER

EIGHT

Syver rubbed his hands down his face, his vision blurring as he tried to focus on the computer screen. The midmorning sun shining off the surface of the countertop didn't help, and he hadn't been able to sleep last night. All he'd been able to focus on was Thea tossing and turning with nightmares. His impulse was to soothe her, to wake her from her fitful sleep and encircle her in his protective embrace.

But he knew she wouldn't welcome such a thing. So he'd just lain awake on the couch and listened, staring at the living room ceiling until his eyes burned.

When she'd finally jolted awake, she'd cried again, and the sound of her almost-silent sobs nearly broke him. He'd seen her cry before, but every time got harder and harder to bear. What else could he do to help her? What could he do when his instinct was to draw closer, but that would only make things worse? He wanted to support her, but how?

Now, some time later, as he worked from home on his laptop in the kitchen, he heard her slippers on the rug before she appeared in the kitchen doorway. He met her gaze from his stool at the counter. She hadn't said anything at breakfast earlier that morning, and she usually shunned his company whenever possible, especially while they were working.

He chose not to speak, fearing she would snap at him—or worse, ignore him.

"Are you busy, or do you have a minute?"

He shut his laptop decisively. They could get mad at him at work for not being available. She was more important. She wanted to talk to him.

Thea crossed her arms and leaned against the doorframe, not attempting to move closer to him. "I want to leave," she said flatly.

Syver's chest tightened, and his breath rushed out of him.

"I haven't decided about whether to go back into the office just yet, but I think I'm ready to return to my apartment at least. I'll come back during the full moons just in case."

He frowned. *I don't want you to go.* He pressed his lips together when the words nearly escaped his mouth. Perhaps it was better for her to leave. He'd lost his cool yesterday, and he still wasn't in control. Plus, as the origin of all her problems, he couldn't comfort her.

"There are some things you still need to know first," he said, glad his voice sounded detached and even, tempered with the thought that he'd known this was coming all along.

Thea raised her eyebrows. "Such as?"

It was surreal to face this conversation, the fact that he could finally explain where they came from, the fact that they were having a calm, easy exchange. He'd tried so many times. By all rights, he should be happy about this development. But given the circumstances, he wished she wasn't ready to talk to him. He didn't want to tell her this last bit. What else would she need from him after this?

Syver sighed. "What do you know about Norse Mythology?"

Thea tilted her head. "You mean like Thor, Odin, and Loki? Only what I've gleaned from popular culture. I think I saw one of the *Avengers* movies a few years back."

Syver shook his head. "Forget all that. Yes, Óðinn, Þórr, and Loki are obviously important and prominent in the old stories, but I'm referring to something else." Syver paused, taking in her stiff stance on the other side of the room. "Would you like to sit down? This may take a while."

"No," she responded coldly.

Syver shrugged as he silenced a sigh. "Suit yourself. According to the sources, the moon and the sun—known as Máni and Sól respectively—are chased through the sky by two wolves—Hati and Sköll."

"You mentioned Hati yesterday as the father of all werewolves."

Syver smiled. As much as she pushed him away, at

least she was listening to him. Thea shifted her gaze to look out the window above the kitchen sink.

"Correct," he continued. "All werewolves—we call them mánagarmar, or moon hounds—are descended from Hati. As far as we can say, Hati had a clutch of children with a serpent of Hvergelmir. The early mánagarmar inherited two things from their parents. The first is venom from their mother, which is why a werewolf's bite is infectious. The second is their father's desire to devour the moon, which is why we cannot stop the change when the moon taunts us the most."

Thea flashed him a disbelieving expression. "We want to eat the moon?" she asked blandly.

Syver shrugged. "So I was taught. I understand it sounds far-fetched to modern ears, but the prophecy says Hati will catch up to Máni in the end."

Thea frowned seriously. "I thought you were going to tell me we had some grand purpose, that some greater good would come out of being a werewolf."

"Who's to say what's good or not? We're manifestations of chaos, of the untamed nature of the wilds. If Hati wasn't chasing Máni, would the moon move across the sky like he's supposed to? Would balance and order exist without darkness and chaos constantly at its heels?"

"So we're the bad guys who keep the good guys running scared? Figures…" she muttered.

Syver released a patient breath. He'd been raised with these stories from an early age. They informed the man he grew into. But Thea had been raised on

American optimism and happily ever afters her whole life.

"Do you know the story of Fenrir, Hati's father?"

Thea shook her head.

"The short version is that Fenrir, who's a child of Loki, was prophesied to kill Óðinn. The gods tried to raise him under their control, but he grew so big and strong that they became afraid of him. Eventually, they betrayed him and tied him up from that fear. Fenrir will have a major part to play in the end of the world. That makes him sound like a 'bad guy.' But would Fenrir have become a bad guy if the gods hadn't betrayed him, hadn't feared him just because he is who he is?"

"A self-fulfilling prophecy," Thea said.

"In this case, yes."

"I get that you're being all philosophical. What is a bad guy, really? What's a good guy? It's all a matter of perspective. You need darkness to have light or whatever mystical shit you're saying. But what does that mean for me? Why does it matter to me? If I'm now an agent of chaos or whatever, why bother keeping my other side in check?"

"Do you want to let your wolf side run amok?" he asked.

"Of course not. I don't want to hurt anyone, especially those who don't deserve it."

Syver nodded. "That's because just as much as your wolf is a child of Hati, your human side is a child of Heimdall."

"Who the hell is that?"

"Heimdall is the watchman of the gods, ever

vigilant. He's the father of all humans. He's the ultimate symbol of order and duty. Therefore, your wolf side and your human side will always be at odds."

"What am I supposed to do about it, then? How do I get any better than I am now? How do you go around without anyone knowing or without accidentally killing your neighbors?"

Syver stared at her for a long time. How many mistakes had he made in his life? How many times had he almost hurt someone? He'd apologized to her for what he'd done. Did she not think it was a mistake? Did she think he'd done it on purpose?

"I've made mistakes," he said quietly.

After a heavy silence, he continued. "I'll tell you what I was told. You must accept that there is chaos and the capacity of ferocity within you. There always has been. Are you so disciplined that you've never said or done anything you didn't want to when your emotions got the better of you? Are you always aware of your every thought and feeling? Of course not. No one is. The only difference is that now that inner chaos has a little more bite. If you embrace it, you can wield it. If you reject it, it will wield you. You have within you the capacity for great love and great hatred, forgiveness and revenge. You must find the balance and decide what to do when. Just know that it is not something that can be smothered or fully controlled. Just like Fenrir will break his tether, so, too, will your inner wolf if you try to control it too tightly."

CHAPTER

NINE

Thea sat with her back against the headboard of Syver's bed, letting the book she held in her hands fall to her lap. After Syver's explanations, he'd given her a stack of books to read. "Eddas and sagas," he'd called them. After she'd logged off her work computer, she'd started reading the *Poetic Edda*, but she could only take so much poetry.

He'd never agreed to her wanting to leave, but he didn't say she wasn't ready either. He'd only said there were things she needed to know, and then he'd told her. Did that mean she could go whenever she wanted?

She hesitated. She wanted to go. She'd wanted nothing else since the moment he'd brought her here. But now that it was a real—a safe—possibility, she wasn't so certain.

She knew if something should happen, if she

needed his help, Syver would come to her wherever she was. That knowledge was both comforting and unsettling.

She wasn't alone. She had someone she could trust to catch her, cover for her, protect her, whatever she needed. But she didn't want to rely on him. The more she relied on him, the harder it would be to leave.

And she needed to leave. He was bad for her in every way she could think of, as if turning her into a werewolf, or a mánagarmr or whatever, wasn't indication enough.

For the first time, she wondered with an open mind why he'd done this to her. She'd asked, or rather screamed, the question at him over and over, but all he ever did was apologize. Was he so lonely that he'd wanted someone with him?

She'd never seen him talk to anyone but the people at work. He never had any personal calls. He didn't even have social media.

Surely, a man like him isn't lonely. He could have any woman he wants… But could he really *have any woman? Oh, he could bed them no problem, but would anyone choose this life? And could he ever have a real relationship without sharing this part of himself?*

Why had he chosen her, only to apologize?

Then again, she'd never understood why he'd chosen her from the beginning, especially since she hadn't been capable of being herself around him back then—too affected by his presence. It wasn't that she didn't think she was pretty or that she had low self-esteem, either. She liked herself just fine. It was that she was just normal, average. She seemed almost dull next to Syver's extraordinariness—or at least she did before.

She couldn't help but remember how she'd felt that first time he'd asked her out.

Thea's cheeks flushed, and an unrestrained smile forced itself onto her face. She scolded herself, peeking over at Syver as the elevator slowly made its way down to the first floor.

Stop smiling like a stupid fool. You're a grown-ass woman, not a giddy schoolgirl with a crush.

But, as always was the case when Syver was around, she couldn't help herself. She had no control over her face at all. And while her insides bubbled with delight like a shaken soda, she knew the minute he was gone, shame and embarrassment would resurface.

Glancing sideways at him again, her flush traveled to other parts of her body. She wondered what his hair smelled like, what it would feel like to run her fingers through it. She would bet her next paycheck he was a great kisser.

Thea forced her eyes forward, shifting her weight uncomfortably. *Oh my God, so unprofessional.*

The elevator dinged, and Thea breathed deeply the fresh air of the lobby as she hurried to distance herself from her fantasies.

"Thea," Syver called out to her, his tone easy and smooth.

A shiver ran down her spine as she halted in her retreat and turned toward him. She flushed anew as she met his green eyes.

"Do you have plans this weekend?"

Thea blinked at him. *Why is he asking? Does he need some reports to complete a work project by Monday?* She didn't have any specific plans, but she didn't want to work either.

He smiled a warm, confident smile.

Then again… She shook her head.

"Then how about joining me for coffee tomorrow?"

Thea's heart squeezed, and her throat tightened. She must be dead and in heaven. Either that or she was hallucinating. She couldn't speak, couldn't form words. Her head spun, and she realized she'd stopped breathing. She gasped softly.

Syver stepped closer to her, her stunned silence not deterring him in the least. "I'd like you to have coffee with me, Thea," he said, his smile at full force, and his eyes fixed on hers.

"I'd like that," she whispered.

When Syver called from downstairs that dinner was ready, Thea put the book and her memories aside for the moment.

Once settled across from him at the table, Thea

stabbed at her bowl of salad—the cherry tomato rolling away from her fork every time she tried to spear it. Giving up, she shoved the lettuce into her mouth and glanced at Syver. He was cutting his chicken breast into even slices.

Crunching on her lettuce, Thea wondered if he would answer if she asked calmly. She swallowed. "Why did you turn me?"

Syver flinched, his hand slipping and his fork squeaking against the glass plate. They both winced at the horrible sound.

He met her gaze, his green eyes flat and guarded.

His silence stretched out, and she looked back down at her plate, her frown weighing her expression down.

"It was an accident," he said.

His words, spoken so softly and with the tone of an apology, stunned her just as much as if he'd shouted them at her.

Thea's stomach dropped, and shame slithered in her guts. She started tapping her fingernail on the table, trying to control her tone. "An accident," she repeated flatly. She clenched her jaw. What had she been expecting? What did she think he would say?

Glaring at him, she stood from the table. She would've been happier not knowing. After taking two stiff steps away, she froze. Then she spun back around, returned to the table, and grabbed her bowl and plate before heading upstairs.

Somewhere in the back of her mind, she told herself that at least he didn't do this to her on purpose maliciously.

But she wasn't in the mood to hear it.

So I'm just a fluke to him, an easy lay that got out of hand, an inconvenience he's now stuck with. I get it. Well, I won't mess up his life anymore. He doesn't owe me anything. I'm not his responsibility.

TEN

S yver blinked, staring at the empty chair across from him where Thea had just been sitting. *What just happened?*

His mind whirled in confusion. He would never be able to erase the memory of the fury and agony in Thea's voice as she screamed "Why did you do this to me?" over and over. After five months of unaccepted apologies, he thought Thea didn't really want to know how she'd been turned.

He'd been surprised at her sudden question— calm and serious in a way she'd never asked before. But he'd followed Rorik's advice. He'd been honest.

He'd turned her entirely by accident though in his darker moments he wondered if that was true. Had he turned her subconsciously? He'd been with many women before her and never turned anyone.

After that bittersweet night, he'd hoped, he'd prayed to Hati and all the gods he could name, that she wouldn't turn. When the full moon had come around, he'd watched for the signs.

He wouldn't have chosen this for her, but something dark inside him had been happy—happy she knew who he really was, happy they shared something, happy she was with him now no matter how enraged.

His current confusion soured as his muscles tensed. *Why would telling her it was an accident make her* angrier? *Why would I have apologized all this time if I'd done it on purpose? Did she* want *me to have done it on purpose against her will?*

He understood her rage at her life being upended. He even understood why she would be mad at him for doing it to her. But this he didn't understand at all. What had she wanted him to say?

He blew a hot breath through his nose and dropped his fork and knife onto his still-full plate with a clatter. *I need some fresh air.*

Syver's chair screeched as he stood from the table. It took him less than five seconds to get to the back deck.

He sucked in the evening air, which did him little good. The sun lit up the trees to the west, nearly to the horizon. It had dipped just below seventy, and the last of the cicadas were singing desperately.

Fury raced through his veins. He wanted to let his wolf run. He wanted to let chaos reign for just a little while. He didn't have to deal with this. It didn't matter what he did; he couldn't do anything right in her eyes. Nothing was good enough.

So why should he keep catering to her? Who made her queen of the world? How many mánagarmar had he known over the years thus far? Had any one of them ever been as moody and hard to please as she was?

He'd been honest. He'd told her truly, and he'd taken responsibility. He'd even apologized countless times and meant it. He'd tried to be compassionate, tried to understand and be there for her. But everything he'd done had only blown back on him.

A man could only take so much.

If she wants to leave so bad, if she's so keen to get away from me, then good riddance. I've done all I can. I wash my hands of the whole thing.

But even as the words ran through his head, fear gnawed at his anger.

He'd done this to her. He'd made her this way. The guilt was heavy to bear, but carry it he must. He had no right to put it down, not while she was still struggling.

He remembered what she was like before.

She'd been sweet, almost shy. He hadn't needed supernatural vision to notice how her cheeks had blushed every time their eyes had met. He hadn't needed the nose of a werewolf to smell the arousal that had warmed her pheromones whenever they'd shared the elevator.

He could still picture her the first day he saw her, the autumn breeze blowing through her hair as she stood in the shade at the company picnic. Even then, yards away, she'd caught his eye. He hadn't been able to take his gaze off her since. And after countless nights of her running through his dreams, he'd decided to ask her out for coffee.

Coffee had turned into dinner, and dinner had become the night that had changed both their lives forever.

Where had things gone so wrong? Memory flooded his brain as he recalled their first conversation.

An unbidden smile spread across Syver's face. *So she works here after all.* Deciding that he suddenly needed a cup of coffee, he rose from his desk chair and made his way toward the kitchenette.

He slowed as he neared the copy machine, taking in the woman who was pressing buttons, a line of concentration between her brows.

He'd seen her at the fall family fun day picnic the month before but hadn't gotten a chance to talk to her. As the new hire, and with the way he looked, most everyone wanted to talk to him. He couldn't get away.

But that hadn't stopped him from noticing her from afar. She'd worn jeans, ankle boots, and a white tee under a long cardigan. She was pleasant looking, with golden brown hair and brown eyes, though he wouldn't say she was a great beauty. She was average in a comforting sort of way, easy to look at. There was nothing wrong with that.

At first, he'd thought she was someone's wife or

girlfriend. He'd never seen her at the office though it was a big building. But the more he watched her, the more his eyes kept returning to her chatting with a blonde woman in the shade of the autumn leaves, the more he found himself hoping she had only come with a friend.

The woman glanced over at him from the copier, noticing he hovered nearby. He flashed her a smile, one he knew never failed to charm. A delicious tint of pink surfaced on her cheeks.

"Hello," he greeted, offering her his hand. "I'm Syver. I don't believe we've met."

She returned his smile, her brown eyes glinting with amber. "Oh! I'm Thea." She let out a little giggle, then bit her lips. "I work in the product planning office. I came down the hall to use your copier. Ours is broken at the moment…" She trailed off, her blush traveling to her ears.

He smirked. He had that effect on most women, and he was glad to see she was no exception.

As she clasped his hand, a jolt ran through him. His vision sharpened, and he looked at her more keenly. He breathed in her scent, memorizing it. He had to force himself to let go.

"Well, I'll leave you to it, then," he said, glad his voice didn't carry any of the surprise and intrigue coursing through him. "It was nice to meet you."

Syver's mind snapped back into the present as the sharp sound of a car door slamming reached his ears.

ELEVEN

Thea glared at Syver's house in her rearview mirror. She blinked hard against the burning wetness in her eyes, telling herself it was from staring too hard and nothing else.

Her insides quivered, and she felt like she was going to throw up. Clenching her jaw, she breathed loudly through her nose.

When she finally drove out of the woods and pulled up to the four-way stop, she forced herself to relax and let the air in her lungs out slowly.

Her vision blurred with tears as a lump formed in her throat. Out in the county at this time of night, there weren't any cars around. Putting her car into park, she took a moment to steady herself.

This was the right thing to do. She had no reason to stay. More importantly, she *wanted* to leave. She couldn't stand to look at him. He'd fucked up her life. So what if he stuck around to pick up the pieces? Did that mean she should forgive him? And then to find out that he'd helped her afterward out of obligation… She hated nothing more than being a burden to others.

All the things he'd done—to think that he'd housed her, fed her, *bathed* her. How many times had she scratched or bitten him while he'd soothed her out of an emotionally driven transformation?

The man must be trying to get into heaven. He'd been patient, annoyingly so, while she'd sniped and raged at him for five whole months.

Well, she wasn't his problem anymore. She could handle it on her own.

The lump in her throat settled in her stomach, and she glanced toward the eastern horizon. The waning moon was large and yellow as it began its evening ascent. She clicked her tongue. It was beautiful and mysterious, and she did sort of have the urge to take a bite out of it.

Her phone vibrated with a call, pulling her from her thoughts. Glancing at the screen mounted to her dashboard, she saw it was her mother calling. She pressed the speaker button and put her car in drive to head home.

"Hey, Mom, what's up?" Thea said, trying to sound as cheerful as she could.

"What's wrong?" Her mother was not fooled for a second.

Thea shook her head with a snort. "Nothing. I'm just tired."

"Are they still keeping you super busy at work?"

Thea squirmed in her seat. She hated lying to her mom, but what could she do?

"Yeah, this project is really taking longer than expected."

"Tell me about it. You only live two hours away, and you'd think you were on another continent for how often we see you."

"It's only for a little while longer," Thea remarked, hoping it was true.

"Do you think you'll be able to come home for Thanksgiving, then?"

"I hope so," she answered noncommittally. "Anyway, what's new with you? I was going to call you over the weekend."

"Oh, I just needed to talk to someone other than your father," her mother said, clearly annoyed.

Thea huffed a laugh. "What did he do this time?"

Her mom made a scowling sound. "He's been practicing his impressions all day. I swear to God, if I hear him say one more thing with the voice of that orange menace, I'll poison his goulash."

Thea laughed.

"It's how I cope!" her father called loudly in the background.

"Well, you can't poison him now. You threatened him out loud. You'll have to wait a few months to throw off suspicion," Thea pointed out.

"Oh, I'm not worried about that. I know I'm your favorite. You'll cover for me," her mother reasoned.

"I've been treated worse than any husband in the history of husbands," her father said in a breathy, gravelly impression.

"Oh my God! Stop!" her mother groaned.

Thea laughed again.

"Don't laugh. You're encouraging him. How do I made him stop?"

"I'm not allowed to speak. They're calling it a gag order. Everyone else is allowed to speak but me. It's my constitutional right, and they've taken it away," her dad continued.

Her mom growled. "Why? Why do men do this? They annoy us on purpose, right? What do they get out of it? Is my impotent rage entertaining to you?"

"Yeah, kind of," her dad said.

Thea bit her lip. "Mom, don't kill Dad. They'll know it was you. The spouse is always the first to come under suspicion. Come on, you watch crime dramas."

Her mom sighed heavily. "Anyway," she shouted over whatever her husband said. "How are you, baby girl?"

Thea smiled warmly. "I'm all right, Mom. Like I said, just busy."

"You're making sure to get enough sleep, right?"

"Yes."

"And you're eating all right? Not just junk food."

"Yes."

"It's starting to get cold out. You're making sure to dry your hair before you go outside?"

"Yes, Mom."

"Don't use that exasperated tone with me. I'm your mother. It's my right to worry about my only child."

"I know. I love you, Mom."

"I love you, too, baby girl. Let me know if you need anything, and I'll talk to you in a few days."

"Yep. I'll call you on Saturday morning."

"Okay. Love you."

"Love you, too. And tell Dad I love him, too."

"Eh, if I feel like it."

Thea chuckled and said goodbye before hanging up.

She felt a little steadier after talking to her parents. Despite the uncomfortable feeling that had settled in her stomach, it was nice to know that some things in the world never changed.

As she finished driving to her apartment, she thought about whether she was ready to return to the office. Thankfully, her supervisor was compassionate and understanding. Of course, Tammy thought Thea was seriously ill. Then again, it wasn't really a lie to say she'd caught something.

Her apartment was quiet and still when she entered without turning on the light. Her night vision was one of the only things she truly appreciated about being a werewolf. She dropped her bags—filled with all of the things she'd taken to Syver's—near the front door before crossing the room and turning on the lamp with the dimmest light.

She flopped onto the couch and let the stillness envelop her in a silent moment of peace. *Now what?*

Her phone vibrated with one short burst. Picking it up from the coffee table, she saw it was a message from her new neighbor.

Do you work on the weekends? Are you free Saturday? I'm craving burgers and onion rings.

Thea smiled, feeling truly normal for the first time in months.

Perfect. Meet in the parking lot at noon?

I'll be there.

TWELVE

The note Thea had left on the kitchen table trembled as Syver's hand shook.

I'm not your responsibility anymore. Sorry that I <u>accidentally</u> became a burden.

His body flushed as his stomach threatened to expel the dinner he hadn't eaten. Pain shot through him, and he started to sweat, a hot flash heating his blood. He recognized the inevitable signs of an emotional transformation, so he didn't fight it.

A strangled grunt escaped him instead of the scream inside his head. He doubled over. His bones melted while his skin itched.

He tried to let go of his human thoughts. This was who he needed to be right now. This was who he was. Sorrow, rage, and an unnamable drive mingled with the agony of breaking bones and tearing muscles.

But after one anguished minute, it was over. He didn't think about what to do; he didn't need to. Wiggling out of his clothes, he ran through the still-open back door.

The night felt warmer with his fur coat. The nighttime creatures fled before him, instinct telling them to get out of the way.

He was quick, as fast as any coyote, while he streaked through the woods and into the tall crops of the surrounding farms. He could hear the farm dogs barking in his wake, but he paid them little mind. He would be gone before the farmers even knew he was there.

The summer was dying, and he could smell the fruit of the fields ripening. But the ground was still warm beneath his paws.

Normally, this was enough—to be wild, to catch a scent and take down a wolf's natural prey. The thrill of the hunt, the chase, the pursuit of something he would eventually catch, it was the best part of being a mánagarmr.

But not tonight. The freedom of shedding his humanity didn't quite stick. He could still feel his sorrow, his rage, his confusion.

What was she thinking? Why did she leave without a word? Does she really believe I think of her as a burden? I've never indicated as much.

She wasn't a burden to him. She never had been. He felt responsible for her, sure. But he'd never felt that responsibility was heavy. As much as he didn't want her to go through hardship, he was also glad that she needed him. He felt strong like he had a real purpose when he was helping her, protecting her, teaching her.

He'd never felt anything like it.

He knew she would outgrow him one day, that she might not need him to guide her as much. But he'd still hoped he could protect and support her. Surely, everyone needed that from someone.

She could leave if she wanted. But he wouldn't have her leave under false pretenses. If she thought she was a burden to him, then he needed to correct that assumption.

As he neared her apartment on the outskirts of town, he deftly dodged porch and street lights. How many times had he sneaked near her place in those early days, watching to see whether she would shift or not? He knew the route, the best way to go about his business unseen.

Slinking to the back of her building, he found her sliding glass door with ease. The blinds were open, and she sat on the couch with her knees pulled up to her chest. She smiled an easy smile as she typed something into her phone.

It was the perfect image of her, comfortable in her own space, in her own skin. His heart squeezed that he wasn't a part of it.

The howl started low in the back of his throat, then elongated into something truly mournful.

She sat up straighter on the couch, her head snapping toward the direction of her back door.

She knew he was there. This was a signal to all mánagarmar. This was how they called to each other. Her instinct would draw her to him.

Thea took two steps toward the door, then crumbled to the floor.

Panic shot through him as she started to convulse. He hadn't thought it would force the change in her. He rushed toward her patio, not thinking about how he would open the door in this form.

But as he neared, the door beside hers opened, and the man who'd approached Thea the day before stepped out into the night.

He scanned the darkness, a wooden rod adorned with metal rings in one hand. His gaze landed on Syver, and Syver skidded to a halt.

They stared at each other in a moment of tense silence.

Syver darted toward a group of nearby trees. He couldn't transform in front of the man, and he couldn't break into Thea's house with him right there. He needed to act as a wolf would.

Syver peered through the branches of the evergreens he was hiding amongst. The man made no move to follow him, just stared in his direction, squinting against the darkness.

Syver shifted his attention back to Thea. She was curled onto her side on the floor in a fetal position. But she hadn't started to shift. As the minutes dragged on, she sat up, then stood—her knees a little wobbly.

She crossed the room and shut the blinds.

Syver weighed his options. Thea's neighbor had gone back inside. If Syver couldn't call Thea to him, then he needed to go to her.

What was the likelihood she'd shut the door in his face when she opened it to find him there naked?

Would her neighbors see him and call the police before she could let him in?

A pathetic whine climbed up his throat.

He needed to clear up this misunderstanding, but she obviously didn't want to talk. She knew he was there and hadn't come out.

If he went home and called her, would she answer? If he texted her, would she ignore it?

Licking his nose, he made his decision.

THIRTEEN

Thea opened her front door, her eyes bulging when she found a stark naked Syver on her doorstep. He stood nonchalantly as if it were an entirely normal thing to do.

"What—?"

He tilted his head and smirked. "Mind if I come inside? I don't want to cause a scene."

She grabbed his wrist and pulled him into her living room before any of her neighbors could see him.

Shutting her eyes, she sighed out a heavy breath as she leaned on her hand, which rested on the now-closed door.

"What the hell is wrong with you?" she grumbled. "You come here, howling outside my window, nearly forcing me to change, and now you just knock on the door butt-ass naked?"

"Well, if someone hadn't left without so much as

a fuck off, we wouldn't be in this situation, would we?"

Thea spun around to glare at him, then averted her gaze away from his full glory. "What did you want me to do? Stick around when you made it clear I was an inconvenience? I'm not so shameless."

"Who said you were an inconvenience? Did I say that? No."

"You—" Her voice came out in a shout. She started again in a hushed tone. "You said you turned me by accident. Was that a lie?"

"It was an accident. But I don't know how you got from 'I fucked up' to 'You're a burden.'"

Thea's chest tightened. "That's right. It was all a mistake. I was a mistake."

"That's not what I said," Syver growled in frustration.

Thea sniffed hard through her nose, forcing her tears down. Straightening her spine, she turned fully toward him and met his gaze. "What *are* you saying, then?"

"Thea," his voice was low and warm as it caressed her name. He stepped toward her, and she stiffened. "You're not a burden. I've never thought of you that way. Yes, I turned you by accident. Why would I do this to someone on purpose? *You're* not a mistake. I *made* a mistake. I…"

Thea's own heartbeat was loud in her ears. She held her breath. "You what?" she whispered, her stomach quivering.

He frowned, a bitter twist of his mouth like he didn't want to finish his sentence.

"You what?" she demanded, her tone harder.

"I lost control, okay?" he snapped. "I've been a mánagarmr for more of my life than not, and I lost control. I shouldn't have. I don't know why, except that I can't think straight when you're around."

Thea blinked stupidly at him, her breath catching.

"T-that's not to blame you," he tripped over his words in his rush to get them out. "I'm not blaming you. You did nothing wrong."

Thea's mind whirled. She scarcely wanted to interpret his words. "Are you saying that being near me makes your wolf want to come out?" she asked quietly.

He ran one hand down his face. This conversation was clearly making him uncomfortable.

"I'm saying that everything about you drives me wild. I can barely function. You know how close to the surface the wolf is when you're off balance. That night…it was the first time I'd gotten so…caught up in someone else. I couldn't help it. But that doesn't mean I'm blaming you. And I'm sorry my lack of control did this to you. The moment I realized how you affected me, I should've run in the other direction. I shouldn't have tried to get close to you. But now it's…too late. I'm sorry."

Thea's heart raced as her body heated. Her tongue darted out to wet her lips, and her breath came out in shallow huffs. "I understand," she said flatly, trying desperately to level her mind as her inner world tilted.

Syver lowered his gaze.

She knew she shouldn't say what she was thinking, that it would only lead to more trouble. She was so close to getting free. But she just couldn't help herself. "I understand because I was the same."

His eyes snapped up to meet hers.

"Do you think I have public sex with every guy who takes me to dinner? I'd never done anything like that."

His expression sharpened, and his manhood stiffened before her eyes. He took a step closer to her, and she didn't back away—not that there was anywhere to go with her back practically to the front door.

"Thea," he murmured, reaching toward her and catching her hand.

A tingle ran up her arm, and she couldn't pull her eyes from his.

She shook her head. "It's not a good idea," she insisted, clutching at the last thread of rationality his touch was urging her to burn.

"Why not?" he asked, crowding her as he stepped well into her space.

"Because. If we can't think straight when we're around each other, then who knows what could happen? Last time, you turned me into a werewolf."

"You called us agents of chaos…" He lowered his head, hovering his lips just above hers. She shivered with need as a painful ache throbbed within her. "So let's be chaotic."

Her will to resist him broke like a weakened string of pearls, and she pulled him down to her, pressing her lips to his as if to devour him.

He pushed her up against the door, his naked flesh as hard and unyielding as the solid wood. His hands burned her through her clothes as they traveled ravenously down her body.

She grew dizzy, drunk on his intoxicating kisses—each one leading her closer and closer to the brink of madness like so many will-o'-the-wisps in the darkest night.

His lips dipped to her throat, and she flinched. She recalled the scrape of his teeth. The pain had been pleasurable during her climax. How she would welcome such pain in this moment as he surrounded her, as his touch demanded that only he exist for her.

And he did. Right now, only his flesh pressed to hers, only the promise of where his rigid manhood would lead mattered.

But she didn't feel the pleasure of his teeth this time. He kissed the spot gently, tenderly, as if he could undo it all and make it better.

Somewhere in her mind, she frowned. She didn't want his apologies or his regret. Reaching down, she wrapped her fingers around his cock and gave it a tug.

He hissed and shuddered against her.

"Show me what it means to be fucked by a werewolf," she demanded, smirking at the desperate panic in his eyes.

With a dangerous grin that made her heart race and her knees wobble, he sharpened his nails and shredded her pajamas. A shiver ran through her as they scraped over her skin—too gentle to leave a mark.

Sensing real peril, real danger at the beast gripping her, her own wolf responded. Her limbs started to shake as her bones heated.

But he didn't stop to let her feel the pain of transformation. Spinning them around, he pushed her down to the living room floor, pinning her beneath him.

His weight atop her was heavy, inescapable in the best possible way.

As she writhed beneath him, her wolf trying to assert her own dominance, he thrust deep inside her. Her muscles seized, and she gasped at the shock as a wave of fervor shot through her.

Now contented with their posture, she clutched at his back, her claws digging into his flesh.

Her moans came out as near howls, ravaging her throat with hoarse tones. Her jaw heated uncomfortably, and her teeth elongated. The feeling of her teeth sinking into the flesh of his shoulder was nearly as exquisite as the sweet warmth of his blood on her tongue.

He grunted and cried out as if her penetrating his skin only added to his gratification.

As he came inside her, she whimpered beneath him, her body vibrating with orgasm.

FOURTEEN

Warmth radiated from Syver's chest, and he couldn't help but smile. If he had a tail, he would have been wagging it.

The sting of the antiseptic Thea was dabbing onto his shoulder wound where she'd bitten him didn't bother him—he barely even noticed its strong smell. All he could think about was how satisfied his wolf felt, how solid her hips were between his palms, and how bright their future was.

"If we get your things out of here by the end of the month, do you think they'll let you break your lease early?" Syver wondered.

Thea's hands stilled. She looked down at him with a frown, his hands slipping from her hips as she stepped out of his reach. "What do you mean?"

"There's no need for you to pay rent for a place you aren't going to be living in."

Her frown deepened. "Who says I'm not going to be living here? I only just got back."

The warmth in Syver's chest cooled. It hadn't even occurred to him that she wouldn't come back with him. Now that they'd made up, now that they understood each other, there was no reason for her to leave.

The thought that she would be isolated, unprotected, this far from him made his stomach queasy. *I need her near me. I can't protect her here.* "I don't like it, you staying here. It's too easy for you to be exposed. You nearly shifted with the blinds open. What if one of your neighbors had been standing where I was? They would have seen you."

Thea crossed her arms, her stance rigid and her expression cold. "I only nearly shifted because you howled outside my window. And the part you're forgetting is that I *didn't* shift. I don't really care if you *like* it or not. You don't get to decide what I do just because we had sex."

Syver flinched, but the pain of her words quickly turned. "Have you gotten into the habit of disagreeing with everything I say? You weren't so obstinate before."

Thea raised her eyebrows. "Before when? Before you turned me into a werewolf?"

"Are you going to keep throwing that in my face? I thought I explained myself. I thought you understood. What was all that, then?" He gestured toward the living room where they'd so recently had the wildest sex of his life.

"That was sex. *Just* sex. You're right. You did explain yourself, and I heard you. We can't control ourselves when it comes to each other, which is exactly why we're not good for each other."

Syver's anger drained away, and he felt like he was going to vomit. "That's not how I see it," he murmured.

"Look at yourself, Syver." Thea flung her hands toward him. "You have claw and bite wounds all over you. And you know as well as I do that we don't heal as fast when our injuries are caused by other werewolves. You want to live your life like this? You want to never have that balance you told me was so important?"

Of course he wanted balance. That was how mánagarmar survived undetected in the modern world. He was just as frustrated as she sounded about her effect on him. But the thought of letting her go was so much worse. How could she talk about it so easily? She couldn't feel as strongly as he did. He wouldn't even be able to say the words aloud.

"I can't," he said weakly. "I can't let you go…"

Her lips trembled, then hardened into a thin line. "As my mentor, are you saying I'm not ready to be out on my own?"

He shook his head.

"Are you planning on keeping me against my will?"

His eyes locked onto hers. Is that how she saw it? "Of course not."

"Then you don't have a choice. I'm not going back. I'm staying here so I can get my life back to some semblance of normal. And I'm going back into the office tomorrow, too."

His skin started to itch as if he would sprout fur at any moment. Somewhere in his mind, he recognized his reaction only supported her argument. He tried to fight it. He had more to say. Surely, there was something he could say that would convince her.

A heavy silence grew between them.

She was letting go; he could see it in her eyes. Her brown eyes, golden with amber, held the sorrow of the death of something great. She was slipping out of his reach.

No.

He stood from the kitchen chair he sat in and took a step toward her, resting his hands on her waist. She didn't loosen in his arms, but she didn't push him away either.

"I won't give up so easily," he said with a self-assured smile, the one he knew set her heart to racing. "You want to find your footing? Get a feel for your new claws? All right. But don't make the mistake of thinking that just because you don't see me, I'm not there. You're going to have to do more than that to get rid of me."

Lowering his face slowly down to hers, giving her enough time to pull away, he kissed her gently on the mouth. "If you want me gone," he whispered, his lips not an inch from hers. "Then you better make me believe it."

He felt the tension in her limbs ease, and he smiled at the effect he had on her. *She still wants me.*

"Call out if you need me," he said low. His grin widened. "Or if you just want another werewolf to get wild with."

Her face flushed as it always did when she was trying to deny her attraction to him.

Willing himself into his other form, he dropped to all fours and shifted. The transformation, while still painful, was much quicker when it was on purpose.

He limped a little from his shoulder wound while he trotted to the back door. He waited patiently as she followed after him to open it for him; she frowned with unease.

As he ran for the cover of darkness, he hoped that unease came from her wanting to give in to him and not her trying to figure out how to finally get rid of him.

I guess bravado was the right word after all.

CHAPTER

FIFTEEN

Thea clenched her jaw and dug her nails into her palms as she stepped into her office. She didn't remember it being so bright and so loud. The fluorescents hummed overhead, joining the cacophony of keyboards, printers, and morning greetings. The smell of her coworkers—all stuffed into their cubicles—mingling with paper and coffee, sweat and aftershave, made her head spin.

She felt the urge to just turn right around and go home. She could easily log into her work computer from her couch. She'd been working from Syver's bedroom for months.

Forcing her jaw to relax, she slowly released the breath she'd been holding. Then she started moving toward her cube.

Her coworkers in the product planning office hadn't yet settled into work and were still greeting each other and pouring their morning cups of coffee from the communal pot in the kitchenette.

She plastered a smile on her face and lifted her hand. "Good morning." She nodded to each person who looked at her.

She wasn't close to any of them, but they were still clearly surprised to see her.

"Thea!" her supervisor, Tammy, called out excitedly, popping her head out of her cube—fancy because it had a door and a window that faced the other cubes.

Thea flinched at the loud enthusiasm though it actually was a normal volume.

Tammy beamed, approaching Thea's desk as Thea put her work bag down. Thea was surprised to see the changes only a few months made in Tammy. She glanced down at her own dress—baggy where it had once been tailored—she'd opted for today. She'd changed a lot, too. It seemed Tammy had decided to go natural with her hair instead of her usual weave. It looked good on her.

"Oh my gosh! You didn't say you were coming into the office today. It's so good to see your face."

Thea nodded and smiled. "Thanks, Tammy. I'm probably still not going to be in the office every day, but it's nice to see everyone."

Tammy lowered her voice as if to shield their conversation from Thea's neighbors—not that it would work. "And how are you feeling?"

Thea unzipped her computer bag. "I'm getting there. Still not 100 percent."

Tammy nodded sympathetically. "All right. I understand. Still, you must be making progress to come all the way here. I'm glad for it."

"Thanks."

"Oh, could you get me that report on the pajama set we were talking about last week?"

"Sure. I'll send it over first thing."

"Great. Thanks."

Thea dropped into her chair, relieved that Tammy wasn't the hovering type. She was a compassionate supervisor, understanding and easygoing, but she also kept things professional. Thea had always appreciated that about her.

Thea took a moment to check in with herself. She'd managed the walk in and the initial check-in with her supervisor. As long as she stayed put most of the day, she should be fine. While the sights and sounds had her feeling on edge, she wasn't in any danger of shifting. She was just used to a quieter atmosphere. She was only a little overstimulated. If she couldn't handle it, she could leave.

"Well, well! Look who's back."

Glancing over, the warmth of genuine joy spread through Thea as she beheld her only work friend, Wheat, leaning her elbow on the wall of her cubicle.

"Glad to see your face. It's not the same talking through chat and email"—Wheat dropped her voice to a whisper—"especially when I can't tell you the real juicy stuff in writing."

Thea chuckled. Wheat always had her ear to the office rumor mill. Thea honestly wasn't sure how the woman got any actual work done.

"So how are you feeling? Better?"

Thea shrugged. "It comes and goes. I'll probably be in and out of the office from now on."

Wheat pouted. "You're my favorite person here. You don't know how hard it's been without you to get coffee with or work out with or eat lunch with. I tried to hang out with Sarah on the social media team"—she shook her head sadly—"and it was not the same."

"I'm sorry to have left you hanging."

Wheat raised her sharp chin, her flaxen hair rippling away from her face. "If you're really sorry, then you'll treat me to something delicious."

Thea pounced on the idea. Eating in her car she could handle. It would be a welcome break in the middle of the day. "Brats?"

Wheat grinned. "Curds instead of fries?"

Thea nodded. "Obviously."

"I'll see you at lunchtime."

After Wheat left, Thea settled into work. It was a little slow-going with all the distractions around her. She felt taut, spread thin, as if anything unexpected would tip her right over the edge. But office life was routine and repetitive if nothing else.

Despite her nerves being on edge, Thea was pleased. She was back to her normal routine. And she felt, if she kept practicing, she would eventually be able to push all the noise to the background as she once had.

Unfortunately, her coworkers—people who had never paid her much mind—seemed to have missed her more than she'd expected. Either that, or they were extremely bored and underworked on a Thursday. Whatever the case, people kept stopping by her cube to welcome her back.

Mike was the eighth such person that morning.

Thea clenched her fists as he showed her pictures on his phone of how much his daughter had grown since she'd been gone. Mike was a nice guy, friendly—a family man. And she used to find the scent of his cologne pleasant. But right now, it was pungent and overwhelming. It was the one unexpected thing she couldn't take at the moment.

"I'm sorry, Mike. If you'll excuse me, I need to run to the ladies' real quick." Thea nearly fell out of her chair, rushing toward the front door of her office as her skin started to itch.

SIXTEEN

Syver gnawed on his lower lip. He'd been a nervous wreck all morning. Thea had said she was planning to come into the office today, and he had no idea how she would handle it.

He felt too far away down the hall in the advertising office. And what was worse, his coworkers kept talking to him.

He'd managed to peek in on her when he'd first arrived. He could see her desk from the entrance of the planning office. She'd looked very annoyed at Bill, who was chatting to her about his recent surgery, but seemed fully in control.

Syver stared at his computer absently, trying to figure out what the curves and lines of the email message meant. He'd tried to focus in on her scent, on the sound of her fingers on the keyboard, but she was too far away. He rolled his shoulders uncomfortably and stood from his chair.

Rishi, the copywriter in the cubicle next to his,

flinched and eyed him when Syver abruptly stood, but he didn't say anything.

I'm just going to pop over on my way to the bathroom—just to make sure she's all right.

Syver forced himself to walk out of the advertising office at an easy pace.

The hallway between their two offices was much too long for his liking, stretching out before him like a path enchanted to never end.

His steps quickened, his throat suddenly tightening at the thought of seeing her. She was pissed at him—what else was new?—but he knew she still wanted him, still needed him…

As he passed one of the conference rooms, he froze.

Panic. Distress. He could smell Thea's usually soothing scent carrying the spicy undertone of alarm and misery. It was closer than he expected. He listened carefully, picking up on her stuttered breathing.

Rushing forward, he opened a closet door to see Thea standing among the shelves of cleaning supplies, her arms around herself. Her eyes widened, and she gasped.

He slipped inside and shut the door, neither of them needing to turn on the overhead bulb.

Syver rushed to her, wrapping his arms around her and pulling her head to his chest.

The fact that she didn't push him away only spoke to how much she was struggling. She was rigid, her limbs trembling in his arms.

He hushed her gently. He didn't need to know

what happened. It could have been anything, and it didn't matter right now.

"Do you hear my heartbeat?" he whispered.

"Yes."

"Concentrate on it." He knew his heart was pounding much faster than was probably comforting, but it would be loud in her ear, an anchor. "Take a deep breath."

She buried her face in his shirt and slowly breathed in through her nose.

"There's nothing here but you and me. You have nothing else to worry about right now."

The shaking in her limbs ceased, and her tension eased as she continued to breathe in his scent and listen to the sound of his voice and the beating of his heart.

His chest warmed, swelling at the thought that in this moment, he was her whole world. He was protecting her in a way only he could.

As the minutes dragged on, the spicy scent of her panic shifted to a warmth he recognized immediately. His manhood stiffened in response to her arousal, to her body pressed against his.

She cleared her throat. "I'm all right now. Thanks," she said, her tone dismissive though she didn't attempt to step away from him.

The dark storage closet suddenly constricted, and Syver felt as if the only air in it was their mingled breaths.

"Are you?" His voice was low and gruff. "I'm not."

She looked up at him, her eyes glinting with amber in the dim light entering from the crack between the door and the floor. Her lips parted ever so slightly, and she released an unsteady breath.

He recognized that tiny opening immediately, having looked for even the smallest signal that his touch would be welcomed every time their eyes met over the last five months.

Unable to resist—all the more from holding himself back for so long—he captured her mouth with his. She tensed in his arms, clutching at his shirt as she pulled him closer.

He stepped forward, pushing her up against the shelves behind her—knocking closed bottles of cleaning fluid onto their sides.

She moaned against his lips, her hands traveling down his torso to unbuckle his belt and unzip his pants. Thoughts of where they were, even what they'd been doing moments before, slipped away from him. All he could think about was how much he needed her.

Lowering his hands, he bunched the fabric of her dress, lifting it above her hips. She was wet. She was ready. He could smell it—the slick heat between her legs would feel so good on him.

Dropping to his knees, he pulled her panties down her legs and buried his face in that sweet taste he'd elicited from her.

She shuddered and smothered a moan, pulling at his hair. He wouldn't stop, not until his name was the only word in her vocabulary.

She kicked her panties onto the floor so she could spread herself wider for him.

He smiled, sucking gently on her clit as he slid his fingers into her.

He could feel his other side edging closer to the surface with every heavy pant of her breath, with every lap of his tongue. He didn't care. It didn't matter. The only thing that mattered was her and the desire he had for her.

"Ah!" she moaned in a breathy whisper. "Please."

He knew what she wanted. All her words from the day before were far away. They weren't good for each other? She wasn't saying that now that she was begging him to fill her.

Standing, he was trying to adjust his hard cock through the opening in his boxers when he heard the distinct sound of someone coming down the hall.

Grabbing Thea from the shelf she'd been leaning on, he moved them to the side of a large metal locker just in time.

"I just need to grab more mirror cleaner," someone said before opening the door to the storage room.

He held his breath, clenching his teeth against the awkward position they were in. Thea had her legs wrapped around his waist, her arms clutching his back. His cock was free, and his pants were slipping from the few steps he'd taken to hide them. Thea shivered, scarcely breathing in his ear.

The custodian clicked on the overhead light, and Syver pressed them even closer into the shadow of the locker.

Every second was an eternity as the janitor puttered around looking for his window cleaner.

"What the…" the custodian muttered, stopping on his way out.

Syver had no idea what had made the man stop, but he didn't dare move to look.

Moments later, he clicked off the light and shut the door.

Syver breathed a sigh of relief, and Thea sagged against him.

"Put me down," she demanded in a low voice.

Stepping back, Syver released her.

Her feet on the floor, she eyed him in the dark, her gaze lingering on his still hard cock. But then she met his eyes with a glare.

"You are ridiculous. I thought you were here to help. I would've been better off if you hadn't shown up at all. I could've gotten through it without almost getting caught having sex in a fucking broom closet. Jesus Christ, Syver. Next time, just leave me be before you get us both fired."

SEVENTEEN

Thea squirmed in the driver's seat, Wheat beside her while they ate lunch in the parking lot. They often ate in one of their cars so they could speak freely without prying ears. As relieved as Thea was to get out of the office, she tried to cling to her anger because she knew an unsatisfied lust she didn't want to address was bubbling underneath.

She couldn't believe she'd let Syver get her into that position at work. Even worse, the janitor had picked up her panties from the floor, and now she had to go commando for the rest of the day.

Wheat was chattering on about all the office drama Thea had missed while she'd been gone. She'd never paid much attention to such things before, and she really couldn't care less now. Her problems were so much bigger than Silvia messing up a contract or Walter getting caught stealing socks.

"So," Wheat said in a tone that drew Thea's

attention. "Are you still seeing the hottie down the hall? You went on a couple of dates before you went on leave, right?"

Thea stiffened, the sweet ache of Syver's tongue on her still too fresh in her mind. "Absolutely not."

Wheat eyed her. "That was an awfully strong response. Did things end badly, then?"

Thea pursed her lips and glared out the window. "You could say that."

Wheat hummed a thoughtful little sound that communicated her curiosity, but Thea chose to ignore it. "All right, then, since it's clearly over between you, mind if I take a swing at him?"

Thea sat up straighter, shifting her gaze to her work friend.

"Or did it end *super* badly, so badly that there are hard feelings? Because I won't if you're not okay with it, but, my God, I'd like to"—Wheat licked some of the mustard that was dripping off the end of her bratwurst—"get my claws into him if you know what I mean."

Thea clenched her jaw, glaring at Wheat's giggling face as a murderous feeling pooled in her gut. "Only if you want to get bitten." Her tone was harsh and sounded very much like a threat.

Wheat flinched and stared at her as Thea chomped down on her bratwurst and chewed with unrequired ferocity.

Wheat chuckled uncomfortably. "Right? I guess he really did a number on you, huh? Well, hey, no worries. If he's that bad, I'll take the warning."

Thea's tension eased, but she didn't feel any better.

There was no reason for her to feel jealous of Wheat even if Syver did go out with her.

What was it to her? They weren't together. She didn't want to be with someone like him.

As she shifted in her seat, their mingled desires, not fully dried on her inner thighs, made her skin stick together uncomfortably.

That man was out of control. He had no regard for either of their careers or what was appropriate in the workplace.

If they hadn't been interrupted, who knows what would have happened? They might've torn the whole place apart. They clearly weren't stable around each other. She was surprised that he'd managed to keep his hands to himself over the last five months—not that she wouldn't have bitten them off had he tried anything.

Still, she couldn't deny there was something compelling, something deliciously dark, something feverishly sexy about what he did to her—and what she did to him.

But so what? She'd never get her life back on track if she couldn't not have sex with him every time they touched. And if she really couldn't control herself, then she needed to cut him out of her life. She would get a hold of this wolf thing eventually. She only had to resist his allure until then.

"So how's your first day back?" Wheat asked, wiping her mouth after swallowing her last bite of bratwurst.

"Actually, I think I'm going to let you out and work from home the rest of the day. I'm really tired for some reason. Maybe the air in the office is too dry."

Wheat nodded sympathetically. "It really is. It gives me a sore throat. Do you remember last winter when I got a bloody nose? We should request humidifiers or something."

Thea agreed, and Wheat continued on with her stories of things Thea had missed.

After they'd finished eating, Thea asked Wheat to tell Tammy she would work from home the rest of the day.

As she drove back to her apartment, Thea assessed her performance. The truth was, even disregarding her liaison with Syver in the closet, she hadn't done well that day. She was disappointed in herself, but she wasn't ready to give up and go back to Syver's. She wondered if there were other ways to practice, other places she could go that were loud but repetitive.

Maybe a café?

She nodded. She'd rather act a little strangely at a café and run out when she needed to than in the office where people knew her and might run after her.

She was so relieved to get home to her quiet, familiar space. She set up her computer on her kitchen table and finished her work with ease. Even the distant sound of her neighbors was nothing compared to the overwhelming clicks and clacks of the office.

Before she logged off at the end of the day, she told Tammy she would work from home again the next day. After considering the problem, she thought that maybe putting an ambiance channel on her television might help—one that had the chatter and beeps of an office environment. If she really felt up to it, maybe she'd light two scented candles with very different smells at the same time.

Either way, she knew she would be safe at home —safe from killing one of her coworkers and safe from her unreasonable attraction to Syver, which seemed to have returned in full force after she'd found out why he'd really turned her.

CHAPTER

EIGHTEEN

Syver stuck his head into the product planning office, his eyes trained on Thea's desk. She wasn't there. Her monitor was off, and there was no laptop in sight either.

Is she all right? She should've been here by now.

"She's not coming in today."

Syver jumped, more surprised by the fact that this human had sneaked up on him than startled by her sudden appearance.

He turned around to find Thea's work friend—he couldn't recall her name—standing behind him in the hallway.

The petite blonde smiled at him, her grey eyes lighting like the sun behind heavy clouds. He knew that look very well, and he wasn't interested.

The woman tilted her head. "Thea told me yesterday that you two weren't seeing each other anymore. Is that not true?"

Syver's gut twisted.

"Oh. I guess it wasn't your choice, then."

He blinked. What expression had he been wearing for her to say that? He smoothed out his face.

"If it makes you feel any better, I'm not sure she's committed to the idea."

Syver analyzed the woman. What exactly had they talked about? What had Thea said? If he asked her friend, would she tell him? Even if she told him, would she then tell Thea about their conversation? Or was she just feeling him out? The way her eyes clung to him, it was clear she was interested in him. How loyal was she to Thea?

Her body language was professional and distant; only her eyes and smile gave her away.

Syver nodded to her stiffly and turned to head back to the advertising office. He wasn't sure what she was really after. Did she want confirmation that he and Thea were no longer dating? He wasn't about to say that out loud.

He very much wanted to know what Thea had said that led this woman to believe she hadn't given up on him quite yet. But he didn't think he could trust her. After all, he'd lived with Thea for five months, and, as far as he could tell, she'd never talked to this woman outside of working hours. Were they even really friends?

Syver felt her eyes on him as he walked down the hall—past the closet where he'd lost control the day before—but he didn't look back at her. In situations like this, silence was the best choice.

Once inside his office, he sighed with relief. Even though he wanted to see her, he was glad Thea wasn't in the office. Objectively, he knew she'd be fine working from home despite his gnawing worry. Maybe he would finally get some work done himself. He'd barely been able to answer emails yesterday from worry and then unsatisfied desire.

Rolling his shoulders, he headed toward the kitchenette. A quick cup of coffee, and then he could concentrate on work.

As he entered, he noted that his coworkers—Mark and Christian—stood near the snack pantry. Christian was showing Mark something on his phone.

They stopped talking for a moment when Syver entered, then lowered their voices—though his werewolf hearing picked up every word.

"I rode the elevator up with her yesterday," Christian said. "What do you think? Should we invite her to my Halloween party next month?"

Syver pulled a coffee mug from the cupboard.

Mark paused. "But if we invite her, she'd probably come with Syver, right? Not that it matters. Looking is free, am I right?"

Syver froze as he reached to return the coffee pot to its warming plate.

"No, dude, they broke up. Wheat told me yesterday."

Rage raced through Syver's veins, and he clenched his fist.

"Oof! Do it. Invite her. Can you even imagine her in something like this tight little devil costume. I'd take an eternity in Hell to see that," Mark commented, gesturing to the phone.

The mug burst in Syver's hand, sending shattered glass and hot coffee all over him and onto the floor. He glared at the two men, whose eyes were wide with shock.

"Do you think this is an appropriate topic for the workplace? I don't think HR would agree," Syver growled, baring his still-human teeth.

His wolf prowled just below the surface of his skin, looking for any excuse to pounce.

Christian sneered. "Looks like someone isn't taking rejection well."

Syver took a menacing step forward. He would rip this tiny human to shreds. He'd take out his organs and feed them to the crows. He'd use his intestines as garlands on his fucking solstice tree.

"He didn't mean that," Mark jumped in. "Getting rejected is rough, man. We get it. We sympathize. Don't we, Christian? We've all been through it."

Syver smiled as a bead of sweat trailed down Christian's face. Despite his sharp tongue, his body seemed to know the danger he was in.

"Right," Christian murmured.

"There's no need to get HR involved. We were just joking around," Mark added, pulling Christian toward the door of the kitchenette. "We're sorry. Aren't we, Christian?"

Christian nodded as they both sped from the room.

Syver shook with residual fury, his wolf entirely unsatisfied—his claws too clean. He stared down at his trembling hands. In the back of his mind, he knew he wasn't in control. He knew this wasn't how a well-adjusted werewolf would act. This was newly-turned behavior. This was the reaction of someone a mentor would never let out in public.

But what was he supposed to do about it exactly? It was clear it wasn't just when Thea was around that he couldn't control himself. It was anything regarding her. Was she right? Should they stay away from each other?

He refused to accept that. No way. Not a chance in Hel.

Besides, she still needed a mentor. She was still struggling. He'd have to figure this out even if it meant quitting his job and going back to Rorik, back to square one. She'd come with him if he said it was necessary.

Looking down at himself, covered in coffee and glass shards, Syver still felt nothing but anger and annoyance at Mark and Christian.

I need to get out of here.

Thea sighed. "Of course it would rain on the last day of summer," she grumbled.

Still, she had the sliding glass door open, the damp air blowing into her house, as raindrops got stuck in her screen door.

The doughnut she was calling breakfast was stale, nothing a dip in hot coffee wouldn't fix. She'd gone grocery shopping late the night Syver had last been at her place. Her mother would be horrified at her choices, but she didn't feel much like cooking.

Why does he have to make everything so much more difficult than it needs to be?

She couldn't get Syver's determined expression from that night out of her mind. And their time in the closet clearly demonstrated he wasn't planning on backing off anytime soon.

Turning him out, pushing him away, had been the most difficult thing she'd ever done, and that was including learning how to be a werewolf.

His eyes on her, his hands on her, made her feel like the most powerful, most beautiful, woman in the world. He gave her confidence and sure-footing.

But how could she ever have a semi-normal life, how could she blend in, when his presence drew out her wolf?

She scowled into her coffee before shaking her head and taking another sip. They would tear each other to pieces. She thought of the punctures her teeth had left in his shoulder; he'd still been bandaged when she'd clung to him in the closet. Hell, they were more a danger to each other when they were getting along than when they were fighting.

Even how her heart had leapt when he'd said he would be there when she didn't see him was dangerous. She didn't have to be afraid of not having support, of messing up so badly that no one could help her. Syver would be there. He'd proven that time and time again. Had he not found her and calmed her down at work?

Her chest warmed, and she coughed to try to shake off the feeling. It wasn't right to rely on him when she wasn't willing to return the favor.

She knew with absolute certainty they were bad for each other. They were a volatile combination, so why had his refusal to let her go only made her want him more? Why had she welcomed his touch the very next day?

It didn't make sense, and that annoyed her.

Her phone vibrated on the table. It was her mom. *Oops.*

"Hey, Mom. Sorry I didn't call yet. I got up late."

That was a lie. She'd been awake all night with thoughts of Syver. She did get out of bed late though.

"No problem. I was about to do some running around, so I wanted to check in with you before I left. What do you have going on today?"

Thea dipped her last bite of doughnut into her coffee before popping it into her mouth. "I've got a new neighbor. We're supposed to go get a burger together."

"That'll be fun. I'm glad to hear you're doing something not related to work for once."

Thea chuckled uncomfortably. "Right? Yeah, he seems nice. He just moved here from Chicago, I guess."

"Oh…? Is that so…?" Her mom's voice took on a suggestive tone. "Is he cute?"

Thea smirked. "He is, actually."

"All the better! You can get yourself a little beef with a side of beefcake."

"Don't say beefcake, Mom." Thea smiled, taking another sip of coffee.

"What? Why not? Are they calling it something else these days? Man meat?"

Thea spit out her coffee, coughing as she nearly choked.

Her mom laughed. "Are you okay?"

Thea coughed some more, trying to get the coffee out of her lungs. "Yeah, I'm fine," she said finally.

"So what are you going to wear on your date?"

Is this a date? Thea thought back to Eero's awkward invitation as she used a kitchen towel to clean up the coffee she'd spit onto her table. *Yeah, I guess it is.* "I'm not sure."

"What's the weather like there today?"

"Upper sixties but rainy."

Her mom hummed in thought. "What about that cute burnt orange dress you have? Remember, you wore it to your cousin's wedding last year?"

"Yeah, maybe." She was sure that dress would be too big on her now. She'd probably just wear a t-shirt and jeans with a tight belt. She hadn't gotten her new clothes in the mail yet.

"Well, I won't keep you. If you got up late, you're going to want to get in the shower soon. Besides, if I leave your dad waiting much longer, he'll get into some project and won't want to go."

"All right. Talk to you later."

"Call me when you get home, and let me know how it goes, okay? And bring that pepper spray we got you just in case."

Thea snorted. She could do Eero more harm than a can of pepper spray should he get out of hand. "I'll call you," she promised.

After saying goodbye to her mom, she downed the rest of her coffee and shuffled toward the bathroom. Her mom was right. She'd need to start getting ready soon if she wanted to be on time meeting Eero.

Thea decided to wear jeans and a t-shirt her mom got her for Christmas under a red flannel, which she left unbuttoned. The shirt read, "I like crime shows, comfy clothes, and maybe 3 people."

Bingeing crime shows together on the weekends

when she was a teen and over breaks when she was in college were some of the best memories she had of her mom.

Thankfully, she had enough time to do her makeup and cover the dark circles under her eyes before her rendezvous. After finishing up with her favorite lip gloss, Thea grabbed her purse and stepped outside her front door.

"This is so convenient," Eero remarked.

She glanced over to see him leaning against the wall between their apartments. He also wore a t-shirt and jeans, making her glad about her choice. His shirt had two crows resting on a twisted tree branch.

She grinned at him. "I like your shirt. What is that? An attempted murder?"

He looked down as if he'd forgotten what he was wearing, then chuckled. "I guess so." He laughed again. "That's Huginn and Muninn."

She tilted her head. The names seemed familiar.

"Odin's ravens."

Thea went about locking her front door. "Ahh. That's right. So I guess not an attempted murder, after all. What's a group of ravens called?"

"An unkindness."

Thea laughed. "Really?"

Eero smiled easily, his eyes warming. "Yeah."

TWENTY

After spinning his wheels contemplating, Syver gave up. If he had any hope of recovering balance, if he had any chance of regaining enough control to prove to Thea they would be good together, he needed help.

Pulling out his phone, he pressed Eilif's name in his contacts.

Eilif was the only skáld Syver knew, and Rorik had often called upon him for situations where he needed wisdom or a knowledge of history.

The phone rang so long that Syver was surprised it wasn't kicked to voicemail.

"Hello?" Eilif's cheerful voice answered finally.

"Hello, Eilif. This is Syver."

"Well, hello, Syver! How are you?"

Syver quirked his mouth. "I've been better. You?"

"I'm fine, just fine. I was just trying to reconcile two contradictory sources for a question that popped into my head overnight. But what seems to be the problem? Anything I can help with?"

Syver smiled. "I hope so. I asked Rorik about it, but he gave me a sort of flippant response."

"That sounds like Rorik. How can I help?"

"I find myself in a situation where I am exceedingly…off balance. My wolf is overreacting to things it normally wouldn't be bothered by."

"Oh? Has something changed in your life? Are you sick? Getting enough sleep?"

Syver sucked his teeth. "More like someone. There's this woman I can't seem to control myself around. Rorik thinks I just like her, but this is getting out of hand. Have you ever heard of this? Is there anything I can do?"

Eilif hummed. "I wonder if it could be related to that…" he murmured to himself.

Syver's heart skipped a beat. "Related to what?"

"Do you remember when we went up north?"

Syver frowned. "I remember the mountains, but I was, what? Nine?"

"You don't remember going to see the vǫlva?"

"No…" Syver tried to recall his time up north. All he could recollect was the bracing cold and the thrilling chase.

"I suppose you were quite young, and it was right after you were turned. In any case, surely you remember the prophecy you were given?"

Unease slithered in Syver's gut. "What prophecy?"

Eilif went silent.

"What prophecy, Eilif?"

The man sighed. "Rorik said he would tell you.

Then again, the 'Hávamál' does warn against knowing too much about your own fate."

Syver's throat tightened, and he cleared it to speak. "Did Rorik take me to a vǫlva for a prophecy about my fate?"

"I mean…he did. But to be fair, you weren't in the room when she spoke the prophecy. Rorik said he would tell you when you were old enough. I just assumed—"

"What did she say?"

"I really think you should call Rorik."

"Rorik has kept it from me this whole time. What did she say, Eilif?"

Eilif sighed heavily. "Let me dig it up for you. It might not even help you with your current problem, you know."

"I still want to hear it," Syver insisted.

"All right. Hold on."

Syver waited impatiently, pacing the length of his living room as he tried to stay calm. He couldn't believe Rorik had kept something this important from him. His palms stung as his nails dug into them.

"Here it is." Eilif clicked his tongue.

"What? What does it say?"

"No," Eilif said, his tone waving away Syver's concern. "She just—it's not even in proper skáldic style. You'd think a vǫlva could've done that at least… though she is usually quite accurate."

"Stop being so prissy, and tell me what it says."

"Excuse me for having professional standards. Fine. She said:

> *A mánagarmr will make*
> *A true oath he will take*
> *Hati mourns his child gone*
> *Hindered from Éljúðnir*
> *The Nornir never err."*

Syver listened carefully, trying to make sense of the words. "'Hati mourns his child gone.' What does that mean?"

"Who knows what prophesies mean before they come to pass?"

"Does Hati's child refer to me since it's my prophecy?"

"Perhaps. Or perhaps it's someone important to you. It could be Rorik for all we know."

Syver's stomach turned. Mourning a child gone in combination with the mention of Hel's hall, Éljúðnir, beyond the corpse gate didn't bode well. *Could Hati's child refer to Thea? She is the mánagarmr I made.*

"That doesn't sound good," he murmured.

"Anything regarding fate inevitably ends in death," Eilif pronounced sagely. "But perhaps being hindered from Éljúðnir means that you will end up in Valhǫll or even Sessrúmnir. Who's to say?"

Syver pursed his lips. Eilif sounded a little too glib when talking about his death for Syver's liking. "And what's the likelihood that I'll die in battle for either Óðinn or Freyja to want me? I have an office job. I'm more likely to drown and end up in the hall of Rán."

His mind turned to a dark place. He lived in America. It was, in fact, more likely that he would be shot at while at work than drown out on the lake. But unless the shooter was armed with silver bullets—the metal long associated with the power of the moon—he was unlikely to actually die.

"Not all battles are fought with swords or guns, especially these days. You can kill people with the stroke of a pen just as easily. In any case, the rules are rarely so clean-cut. If Freyja or Óðinn want you, they shall have you," Eilif responded.

Syver quirked his mouth. There was no arguing with that, but the skáld's logic did little to assuage his unease.

"Okay. Fine. Can you text me a picture of what you just read me? I'd like to think about it more."

Eilif hesitated. "I really don't think I should… Óðinn says in the 'Hávamál' it will only bring you sorrow."

"Óðinn also spends how much time and energy not only trying to learn about his fate but trying to avoid it?" Syver shot back.

"Well, then, he should know how much sorrow it brings."

"For the love of—Just send it to me, Eilif! You already read it to me. What's the difference now?"

"I suppose I should've thought of that. You know, this never would've happened if Rorik had told you like he said he would."

"I agree. Let's blame Rorik. Now, will you send it to me, please?"

"I will. But I really must caution you not to become obsessed with it. The fact is we don't really know what it means."

"Noted. Is there anything else you can tell me about my problem with this woman?"

"There's nothing that I know of from the sources or folklore. Maybe ask Oceanne? She's been in more relationships than any of us combined."

Syver clenched his jaw. He really didn't want to call Oceanne. He couldn't even believe Eilif had suggested it. Then again, Eilif had always been so wrapped up in his books, he probably had no idea about him and Oceanne.

"I'll think about it," Syver murmured. "Thanks for the information."

TWENTY-ONE

Thea and Eero ordered what they wanted from the waitress outside Thea's car. The Stop was as crowded as it always was on Saturdays, the drizzle not discouraging anyone.

"I've never been to a drive-in," Eero admitted. "Do they really put the tray on your car like in *Happy Days?*"

Thea smiled over at the man. "Yep."

"Cool." He grinned, giving her a Fonzie thumbs up.

Thea giggled. *What a dork.*

"Thanks for making time for me," Eero said. "You mentioned you've been busy."

"What kind of Midwesterner would I be if I didn't welcome a new neighbor?"

"Got to love that small town hospitality."

Thea scowled exaggeratedly. "Our city isn't small."

Eero shrugged. "It is compared to Chicago."

"Point taken."

"So what do you get up to out here in the boonies?"

Thea laughed. "Is this going to be a thing?"

Eero smirked.

"All right. Okay, then. We'll see," she answered in a tone that accepted his challenge. "I promised I'd show you around. We can go for a drive after we're done eating. As for me, I mostly just work."

That wasn't quite true of late, but it was nice to talk of the before-times.

"What do you do?"

"I'm a product planning analyst for Yawkie."

He blinked. "What does that mean? You get discounted underwear?"

Thea laughed again. "It means I got a bachelor's in business administration and had to put it somewhere. But, yes, in fact, I do get discounted underwear. What about you?"

"I'm a waste management specialist."

Thea raised her eyebrows.

"I drive the garbage truck."

"Oh, wow. Well, thank you for your service."

His lips twitched into a sardonic smile. "Sure."

"No, I'm serious. That's a really important job."

His expression warmed. "Thanks."

Their conversation halted as the waitress arrived with their food. Thea watched Eero pop an onion ring into his mouth and then close his eyes and moan.

"Right? I told you, didn't I?" Smiling, she bit into her cheeseburger.

After eating their cheeseburgers and onion rings, they sat sipping their homemade root beers.

"So do you only like crime dramas, or are you interested in true crime as well?" Eero asked.

Thea tilted her head, and he gestured toward her t-shirt.

She nodded and huffed a laugh at herself. "I like true crime, too."

"What about unsolved mysteries?"

"The show or the concept?"

Eero shrugged. "I don't know. Both."

"I like a good mystery whatever form it takes. What about you?"

"Me, too. In fact, I've been trying to get to the bottom of a mystery since I moved into the apartment building. I think I finally solved it."

"A mystery in our building? What is it? Who keeps not cleaning out the charcoal grill?"

Eero shook his head. "No, but I'll be on the lookout for that one next. Apparently, the woman who was in my apartment before me—"

"Mrs. White."

"—Mrs. White, then. Well, apparently, she saw something that made her break her lease, and that's why the apartment was available. The guy on the other side of me was telling me about it the day I moved in."

"What did she see?"

"He told me he went into the office to pay his rent, and she was screaming about a rabid wolf—said she saw it dragging a baby deer toward the building."

All the blood drained from Thea's face.

"I know, scary, right?" he continued. "Apparently, Mrs. White had the habit of making up stories and complaining to management, so my neighbor speculates that it was a relief for them to get rid of her. But then, the other night, I heard a wolf howling, and I went outside and saw it."

Thea's eyes bulged, and her stomach rolled. "You did?" she asked breathlessly.

He nodded. "Cool, right? I didn't even know there were wolves in Wisconsin. Coyotes sure, but full-grown wolves?"

Thea forced herself to swallow, her mind whirling so fast she couldn't think of what to say.

"Hey," he said softly. "I didn't scare you, did I? I'm sure it's safe. It's probably not really rabid. I mean, it ran away the minute it saw me."

Thea nodded and tried to smile. "Yeah, I'm sure you're right. I knew there were wolves in Wisconsin, but not this far south. We should probably report that to the DNR or something. Don't they keep track of that stuff?"

"Yeah, maybe. I just thought it was interesting. You hear a story from an unreliable source, and it seems crazy. But lo and behold, it's true. Be careful not to take your trash out after dark, I guess."

"I guess so."

Thea went silent. What had happened that night while she was fighting the shift? Syver had said he'd seen her through her door. Had he rushed to help her only to be seen by Eero?

Her gaze flicked to Eero in her passenger seat. *He*

didn't see me struggling, right? Surely, he would've mentioned it or at least asked if I was all right.

She pictured their back porches. If he'd stayed on his patio, there was no way for him to see into her living room.

"Well, what do you say we take a drive, huh?" she asked, forcing a cheerful tone. She could talk about this later with Syver if she thought she needed to.

"Let's do it," Eero replied. "Show me all the best spots."

Thea pointed out her favorite places in town. She drove down to the lake and showed him the farmer's market, taking up a whole street since it was Saturday. Then she took him by her favorite bookstore and her favorite café before driving by the museums and library. Afterward, she headed north to show him her favorite park and nature preserve. She even passed her favorite shawarma place.

"I guess there's a lot to do in the boonies, after all," Eero said as she pulled into the parking spot nearest her front door.

She rolled her eyes but smiled. "Still going on with that? We have a population of nearly one hundred thousand, you know."

He waved his hand away as if to say that were peanuts.

After climbing out of the car, they stood on the sidewalk between their apartments.

Eero shoved his hands into his jeans pockets and rocked on his heels. "I had fun today. Thanks for showing me around."

Thea smiled. "Yeah, me, too." And she was telling the truth. Overall, her date had been perfectly normal. Eero was funny and cute and easygoing, just the type of guy who would keep her calm and collected.

Eero met her eyes and smiled that endearing, awkward smile. "Next time is on me, okay? You can tell me the best place to order pizza, and maybe we could watch one of your murder shows. I think there's a Poirot movie that came out on streaming recently."

Thea grinned. "Who could say no to Agatha Christie?"

Eero beamed. "Right? She's my in to every woman's heart."

Thea raised her eyebrows. "Oh, collecting women's hearts, are you?" she teased.

He chuckled, quirking his mouth. "Not successfully. Maybe I should try a different approach, actually."

"You're doing just fine," Thea encouraged.

Eero's smile lit up his face. "Well, then, I should say goodbye so as not to ruin it."

Thea nodded. "All right. You have a good night."

"You, too." With another smile and a wave, Eero turned and headed into his apartment.

Thea did the same, shutting the door behind her.

She felt good, calm, normal. Setting her purse down, she thought that someone like Eero was good for her.

Before she could move farther into her apartment, a rapid knock sounded on the door.

She opened it to find Eero standing there. Thea tilted her head. "Did you forget something?"

He nodded. "Yeah," he said, slightly out of breath.

She waited as he ordered his words.

"Can I kiss you?" he asked finally, his determination boyish somehow.

Her chest warmed pleasantly. "Sure," she agreed.

Taking a step into her apartment, Eero fumbled, seemingly not sure what to do with his limbs. As she wrapped her arms around the back of his neck, he settled his hands on her hips, dipped his head, and pressed a light but lingering kiss on her lips. "Thank you," he murmured, his eyes sparkling down at her like seawater in the sun.

Standing on her toes a little, she pecked him again. "You're welcome."

Eero's grin couldn't have been any wider. "Tomorrow night? Pizza and Poirot?"

Thea nodded and released him. "Six?"

Removing his hands, he stepped out of her space. "Six at my place."

Glowing like the midsummer sun, Eero headed back toward his apartment, a bounce in his step.

Thea shook her head with a smile and shut the door again. Her limbs felt light and her body buoyant. There was no hint of her other side.

As another knock sounded at her door, she chuckled, wondering what Eero had forgotten this time.

TWENTY-TWO

S yver tapped his fingertips against his thigh as he waited for Thea to answer the door.

When the smile she greeted him with was warm and welcoming, his heart skipped a beat.

But that smile slid from her face not a second later. "What do you want?" she asked coldly.

His heart sank. "I need to tell—" He froze, sniffing deeply. He stepped into her apartment and closer to her, taking a deep breath.

It smelled like vanilla cappuccino, amber, and male arousal. He didn't recognize the scent. He scowled.

"Who's been in here?" he demanded, white hot anger rushing through him.

Thea stood up straighter. "I don't think that's any of your business, do you?"

His face grew hot and his muscles tense as he clenched his jaw and fists. Thea shut the door behind him while he prowled around her living room, sniffing to discern how far the intruder had infiltrated.

"I don't recall inviting you in," she snapped.

"What's going on? Did someone come here? Why do you smell like male lust?"

Thea's face flushed, and she squinted. "I had a date if you must know."

Syver's stomach dropped, then hardened. *A date? Is she serious? It hasn't even been a week since we were rolling around on this very spot.*

"Are you insane?" he growled.

She bared her teeth at him.

"Do you have any idea how much you're playing with fire?"

She put her hands on her hips. "So I can't date now?"

"What are you going to do if you start to shift around him? What if you bite him? You could expose all of us. You could turn him."

"I'm not you," she sneered. "I can control myself."

He smiled menacingly. "Oh, yeah? Like you controlled yourself in the storage closet."

She huffed an angry breath through her nose, closing the distance between them to point her finger in his face. "Well, lucky for me, he's not an arrogant, overbearing, head-up-his-ass werewolf! So I should have no trouble."

Syver covered the hand she had pointed at him with his and lowered it. Her eyes flashed, and desire squeezed his balls. She could call him whatever she liked, but they both knew how he affected her. The moment they touched they couldn't help themselves.

"Let go," she said, her words far more demanding than her tone.

"Is that what you want?" he asked, sliding his free hand to the base of her back and pulling her against him.

"Yes," she hissed.

Syver smirked, lowering his face toward hers. He would blot out any memory she had of this other guy. He would cover his scent with his own as if it had never been there.

"Really?" he rumbled, his lips hovering over hers as she quivered against him.

She didn't speak; instead, she tilted her head upward, parting her lips in an invitation.

He captured her mouth in a ravenous kiss, and she whimpered, begging him for more. He pulled back, releasing her like he'd just thrown a bucket of cold water on her.

Her expression, which was soft with sleepy desire, tightened into rage. She wiped her lips, but she couldn't remove the scent he'd left there so easily.

"Who do you think you are?" she growled.

He snorted. "Who am I? I'm the arrogant, overbearing, head-up-his-ass werewolf you can't seem to stop wanting."

"So what? Do you think I can't stay away from you? Did I come to your door to beg? No. I had a perfectly lovely afternoon with Eero. It was pleasant and normal and sweet, and I could happily spend the rest of my life in that place."

Eero. The sound from her lips etched the name

into his mind, burning like it was emblazoned with hot iron.

"Is that what you want? Pleasant, sweet, *normal?*" he spat. "You want a human life. Well, you can't have one. If you don't accept that, you'll end up hurting your perfect little Eero."

She flinched as if he'd slapped her. He hadn't meant to be so harsh. But this was her reality now. She was trying so hard to bury her wolf; it would inevitably break its chain and go on a rampage. He'd seen it more than once.

"You're right," he admitted with a sigh. "I can't give you sweet or normal. But I can give passion. I can give you extraordinary. I can understand you in a way he, or any human for that matter, never can. I can meet you where you are. I can protect you. I can be your equal. You never have to be careful with me, never have to worry about hurting me. I swear on Freyja's tears for her lost husband, I'll give you a love for the ages, a love the skáld will write poetry about."

Her eyes flickered with hesitation.

He'd said it. He hadn't planned to, but there it was. Sick with worry over the prophecy Eilif had sent him—convinced that the child of Hati who would become a wandering soul was her—then goaded by another man's scent on her, the oath had just slipped out of him. And he'd meant every word.

"Why do you always have to be so dramatic? You…you're just…too much." The weight of his words seemed too heavy for her as she shook her head. "I can't deal with this right now, not on top of everything else. I'm trying to get my life together."

As much as he wanted an answer right now, as much as leaving his heart exposed and vulnerable felt unnatural to him, he tried to understand. This was overwhelming for him, too. *She* was overwhelming. And he wasn't even dealing with being recently turned.

He dipped his head in a solemn nod. He would wait. He had no other choice. If he pushed her too hard, he could lose her forever.

"Just promise me two things," he said.

She frowned but waited for him to continue.

"Promise you won't hesitate to rely on me for anything werewolf related or otherwise."

"I'll call you if I have problems or questions about being a werewolf," she agreed.

Taking her hand in his, he laced their fingers together, willing her to see his sincerity. "Promise me you won't sleep with this guy until you give me a proper answer. I won't be able to keep myself in check if I think of you as mine and he touches you."

Thea sighed through her nose and averted her gaze. She shrugged her shoulders ever so slightly, and Syver took that as a grudging yes. He could handle no other answer.

Her eyes flicked back to his. "Why are you here anyway?"

Now that he could see she was in one piece and in no perceivable danger, he hesitated to tell her. He shook his head. There was no need for her to worry about a prophecy that might not even apply to her. He would watch over her and think on it more.

Pulling her into an embrace, he whispered, "I just wanted to make sure you were okay."

CHAPTER

TWENTY-THREE

T hea squirmed as she stood on Eero's doorstep. She could still feel Syver's arms around her. He'd held her so tenderly—so lovingly—as if he needed to protect her from the world.

Was he just trying to manipulate me into doing what he wants? Or were the words he spoke last night true? "A love for the ages…" That's quite the declaration.

But still, she hesitated. Despite how her heart had glowed in that moment, despite how the sweet words of acceptance tasted on her tongue, she couldn't bring herself to tell him yes.

The fact was it had been his sweet words, his irresistible charms, that had led her to this place. If she'd refused him before now, she wouldn't be a werewolf. If she didn't refuse him now, what other catastrophes would he unwittingly lead her into?

Between the two of them, one of them had to think clearly, and it obviously wouldn't be him.

She shook her head. *A love for the ages… Who talks like that anymore?*

Rolling her shoulders, she tried to forget his gentle embrace, an embrace that spoke of love and home, comfort and safety, rather than the passionate flame that burned inside her every time he got close. She wasn't used to it, and in the back of her mind, she worried that this side of him would be even harder for her to resist.

Eero opened his front door with the expression of a dog whose person had just returned home from work.

"Come in." He stepped aside with a grin.

"Thanks," Thea said, trying to match his smile but failing.

As expected, his apartment looked much the same as hers. She entered the living room and could see the dining room, which led to the kitchen. To the right was a hall she knew led to the bathroom and bedroom.

Unlike her apartment, which was cozy and comfortable, his was rather scant. He had only a couch and a television in the living room. His dining room table was cafe-sized with only two chairs. The dining room also had a sideboard, which drew her attention as it was the only thing decorated in the space.

She couldn't see it in detail from where she stood, but she saw there was a vase with bright, autumn-colored flowers. She could smell their fresh petals from where she stood.

"So what do you want on your pizza?" Eero asked, taking his phone out with an easy smile.

She told him that she liked the meat lovers—a new favorite of hers of late—and suggested where he should order it from.

As he went about calling the pizza place, Thea drifted about the room, drawn to the sideboard for a closer look.

The surface was cluttered but not haphazardly so. There were tall wooden statuettes with primitive rough features, a vase of flowers, candles, a delicate tea cup, a short staff, and a photo frame.

The wooden staff was about two feet long with a sort of oblong cage on one end—similar to a distaff used for spinning. The cage had brass rings hanging from it and a knob on top.

The frame held the picture of a woman with long golden hair, blowing in the wind as she looked behind her at the camera. Her eyes shined as she laughed, and Thea couldn't help but smile with her.

Eero approached her where she stood in his dining room. "The pizza should be here in about forty minutes. What do you think? *Murder on the Orient Express*, *Death on the Nile*, or *A Haunting in Venice*?"

"Who's this?" Thea asked, gesturing to the woman in the frame.

Eero's smile faltered. "That's my mother."

His eyes wilted with sadness, and a heavy sympathy pressed on Thea.

"She was killed by a drunk driver a few years ago." His voice was steady, but his expression was haunted.

Thea's heart sank. She couldn't imagine how hard

it would be to lose her mother in that way. "I'm sorry to hear that," she said, reaching out and resting her hand on his upper arm.

He smiled sadly at her. "Thanks. She was really special, and she taught me a lot."

Thea mirrored his smile. "Mothers are good that way."

He huffed a laugh through his nose and nodded. "Yeah, I guess you're right. In any case, she wasn't the brooding type, and she wouldn't want me to be either."

"Would you like to tell me about her?"

He met her gaze. "Maybe another time."

Thea nodded. "All right. Anytime you want. What were my movie choices again?"

Eero listed them off, and Thea chose *Death on the Nile*. She'd heard that the cinematography was really good, and she'd already seen the remake of *Murder on the Orient Express*.

After drawing the blinds, Eero settled beside her on the couch, and as the opening credits began, a feeling of effortlessness settled over her. *Yes, that's it. Eero is easy to be around.*

Her thoughts drifted as the images on the screen passed unmarked. She couldn't even imagine what it would be like to sit and quietly watch a movie with Syver. Even their coffee and dinner dates had been wrought with tension. His presence was just so overwhelming. Of course, at the time, she'd been more flustered and shy, but that was before she'd been emboldened by his kiss.

Thea jumped when she felt Eero's calloused hand rest over hers. She glanced over at him.

"Is this okay?" he murmured.

His hand was warm and comfortable. Pleasant really was the perfect word for him. Smiling over at him, she laced their fingers together with a nod.

Then they both turned their attention back to the screen.

Not far into the movie, the pizza arrived. And the rest of the evening was effortless and relaxing—just what she needed to counter the chaos her life had become.

CHAPTER

TWENTY-FOUR

Syver lay in bed, staring up at the ceiling. He'd slept like shit and didn't feel like getting up. It was Sunday, and Thea was no longer in his house, so there was no reason for him to get up anyway.

He knew he should tell Rorik that he'd made an oath. But then again, what was the point? It would only worry the man. And as Rorik had said before, it was inevitable. Knowing now that there was a prophecy, he understood why Rorik had said that. Fate was not a thing one could change or get out of. Besides, he didn't regret speaking an oath to Thea. Not one bit. He'd never been more serious about anything in his life.

On the other hand, by making an oath, he'd just pushed fate one step closer. And if the prophecy's reference to Hati's child was Thea, he'd pushed fate closer to her.

He'd read and reread Eilif's text over and over

until his cellphone had to be plugged in from lack of battery, until his eyes had burned from staring at the screen too long.

The only things he was sure of were that he would turn someone, and he would make an oath. There were no other conditions to the prophecy being fulfilled. The only thing he could do now was try to protect Thea as best he could.

On that point, he was at a complete loss. He'd offered her his everything and could only wait for her to answer. He could potentially work on controlling himself better when it came to her, but the only place he knew to turn to for advice was Oceanne.

His stomach twisted at the thought, and he was glad he hadn't gotten up for breakfast or lunch. He hadn't seen or talked to Oceanne for at least ten years, but he still remembered the last words he'd said to her. *No, I can't call her.*

It was the last night of Sigrblót, and the early spring night had none of the warmth of summer's promise. He hadn't been home for a while, but Rorik had insisted that this was his last blót before graduating college, and he needed the blessings of victory.

He felt her approaching even before he heard her. Syver steeled himself.

"What do you want, Oceanne?" he asked coolly.

"I haven't seen you in a while," she purred.

Syver frowned severely, giving her no safe harbor. "That was on purpose."

Oceanne flinched, her blue eyes wavering as she bit her lower lip. "I know you don't see me the same way I've always seen you."

"If you know, then why do you keep trying?"

Her eyes filled with tears. "Do you think I want to be this way? Do you think if it were so easy to give up on you, I wouldn't have? I can't help it! When I'm by myself, when I'm around other people, other wolves even, I'm fine. But if you're there, I just… I can't seem to think straight. It's like I lose myself entirely. I know you've never looked at me that way. You think I don't know? How could I not know?" she wailed, shaking as she wrapped her arms around herself.

Tears streamed down her objectively attractive face, a face that had never once tempted him despite her best efforts.

"P-please, Syver. Have pity." She reached toward him, but he stepped away. "Just once, just one night. Give me this one night, and it will carry me through a lifetime."

Syver stared at her. He did pity her. She was a mess. She became a totally different person when he was around. He'd seen it from afar, heard others whisper about the changes. And that was why he knew he couldn't give in. These feelings for him, this obsession, would only get worse if he relented even a little. Could she really not see that? Refusing her was the best thing he could do for her.

"Get a hold of yourself," he said. "Have some self-respect. Do you know how pathetic you look? I thought you were better than this." Turning away, he didn't look back even as her sobs tugged at his heart.

"You have no shame," he muttered to himself as his thumb hovered over Oceanne's number in his phone. And he didn't. He'd endure much worse if it meant he could convince Thea.

Clenching his jaw, he pressed the call button. Every ring was like a hammer on an anvil.

"Well, well, well, look what the troll dragged in," Oceanne said, her voice a little older but much sharper. "You've got some nerve calling me."

"How are you, Oceanne?" he asked, his voice even but hesitant.

"How am I? Like you've ever cared. What do you want, Syver?"

Syver knew for certain that this wasn't a good idea. "Before…how you felt about me… What was it like?"

"What?" she responded flatly. "What do you need? An ego boost? State your purpose for this call."

Syver sighed. "I…met someone. And I can't seem to control myself when she's around. Everything feels heightened, and things that normally wouldn't send me over the edge do. She's…adverse to indulging in this with me. She'd rather have a calm life…a human life. So I thought…"

"You thought since what you're going through sounds like what I described to you back then that I'd know how to control it—since I've had to move on with my life when you rejected me?"

"Yeah…"

He could hear the smile in her voice as she continued. "Sure, I know how to control it now. I've let you go and gotten that self-respect you so helpfully pointed out I lacked. Here's what I'll tell you: I hope she rips your heart out and burns it. Then I hope Loki eats it and begets a brood of monstrous offspring that will torture you for the rest of your life. As far as I'm concerned, the chicken has come home to roost. I hope its crow wakes Garmr and his howls drive the wolf inside you mad until you destroy yourself and everything you hold dear."

His phone beeped in his ear. Oceanne had hung up.

TWENTY-FIVE

"What do you say next weekend we go for a hike? I hear it's going to be nice," Eero asked Thea as she readied to leave for the night.

She thought about it, wondering if her other side would have an easier or harder time in the mild wilderness of the park. The gentle lull of nature would certainly be easier to deal with than the loud and unexpected noises that surfaced from being around humans. But then, the scents of wild animals were sometimes harder to resist than any random smell that wafted her way from populated areas.

Eero's blue-green gaze watched her response, unrestrained hope pleading in his eyes.

"Yeah, okay. If I'm not too tired from work. Otherwise, you can come over to my place for a movie, and we can order Chinese this time."

I'll drive up to the park myself during the week to see how I fare first.

Eero beamed. "Sounds like a plan."

"Thanks for the pizza," Thea said.

"Are you sure you don't want to take some home with you?"

"Because four slices wasn't enough?"

"I like a woman with an appetite though I don't know where you put it all."

Werewolf appetite and metabolism were something else, to be sure. She couldn't imagine how high Syver's grocery bills had been while she'd stayed with him.

Her easy smile faltered. There she went again, thinking about Syver while with Eero. Stepping nearer to the man in front of her, she moved to give him a hug.

Wrapping his arms around her, he nuzzled into her, resting his cheek on her head. She gave him a squeeze around the middle as if in defiance of the wolf who wasn't even there.

Pulling back a little, she gazed into Eero's eyes. As she released his torso, she placed one hand on his chest and lifted the other to his face.

He leaned his cheek against her palm with the most endearing warmth in his eyes.

Why was her heartbeat so steady when he looked at her like that? He clearly liked her. If Syver had looked at her like that on their second date, she would've lost her mind.

Standing on her toes, she pressed a kiss to his lips, wrapping her arms around the back of his neck to deepen it. His hands trailed up her back, pulling her against him.

She pushed harder, willing her body to respond as she felt his manhood stiffen. Nothing. Nada. Only the barest hint of arousal on her end. It was there, but it was the normal amount she got from kissing someone. It wasn't even comparable, not even in the same league, to what she felt around Syver. A touch of his hand produced more of a reaction from her.

Breaking their kiss, she took in the drunken smile Eero gave her. "Wow," he breathed.

The senseless word from his lips almost made her feel like she was doing something wrong.

"I'll text you," she promised before wishing him a goodnight.

As she made her way between their two apartments, she argued with herself. It wasn't that she wasn't attracted to Eero. She wasn't a cold fish. It was just the normal amount, the right amount, that allowed her to keep her wits about her.

What was so wrong with that? That was what she wanted, wasn't it?

Letting herself into her apartment, she went about getting ready for bed. She wasn't tired, but the routine was soothing.

Eero was cute. He was kind. He made her feel good about herself, and he made her feel like she was in control. She would spend next weekend with him and maybe even the weekend after that. And nothing and no one would stop her because why shouldn't she?

After crawling under her covers, Thea leaned over to turn out the light.

Yes, this is what I want.

Once plunged into darkness, it took her new night vision only a second to adjust. But as she closed her eyes and willed her muscles to relax, it was Syver's heated smile that flashed in her mind.

"Is that what you want?" he said, sliding his free hand to the base of her back and pulling her against him.

Her body flushed just to think of it. She trembled with the need to feel him against her now.

"Yes." She heard herself say in her memory. Though she'd said so, the word carried no weight in her heart.

Syver smirked in her mind's eye, that irresistible quirk of his mouth that bespoke his intention. He knew she wanted him. He knew, and he would give her exactly what she craved if she was brave enough to let it happen.

"Really?" he rumbled, his lips hovering over hers.

Thea blew out a sharp breath. What had she ever done for her to deserve such an outrageous life? Had she not studied hard, followed the rules? Had she not been a good and obedient child, kind to animals and the elderly? Had she not stayed away from drama at every turn, even distancing herself from high school and college friends when they had become too much?

So why? Why couldn't she leave this man be? Was it because he wouldn't let go like everyone else had in the past? Was it because he was so persistent?

Even as annoyance bounced off the walls of her mind, her body craved the feel of him. If she called to him now, he would come. He would satisfy her in a way only he could.

Squeezing her eyes shut, she bit her lip. She could practically hear him breathing, hot and heavy, in her ear. She could feel him taut against her. Slipping her fingers into her panties, she could feel that she was wet and ready, swollen and throbbing.

His name played on her tongue as she pleasured herself to the thought of him inside her. But she wouldn't say it. She would think it. She would scream it in her mind. But she couldn't bring herself to speak.

TWENTY-SIX

The ground, soft from the day's rain, squished beneath Syver's shoes as he ran. His heart pounded while his lungs sucked in air. This was what he needed.

Here, among the autumn trees, he was in control. Despite the mud, this was solid ground.

Thoughts and worries raced through his mind, but the motion of his body as he ran on the narrow trails gave him a feeling of action.

He wasn't on solid ground with Thea. Perhaps if he had her word that she was with him, that she would stick around and figure this all out together, he wouldn't feel so vulnerable, so unstable. It didn't help that this Eero, whoever the hell he was, was skulking around.

He worried about the prophecy, worried he'd messed up Thea's life even more than either of them thought or could imagine. It was too late to change it now, too late to protect her by distancing himself—

the conditions had already been met. He worried that if she said no to his declaration, he would end up going through whatever Oceanne had. The fact that she was still angry this long after he'd rejected her only hinted at the pain she'd endured.

His fears gnawed at him. And his instinct was to not leave Thea's side until he figured out what the prophecy meant or until she fully rejected him.

Stepping back was not in his nature. But pushing forward, forcing the issue, was doomed to have the opposite effect. She might still want him despite his overbearance now, but what happened when he really pressed?

He had to get control of himself. He had to prove to her that he could be stable for the both of them even when she felt overwhelmed.

Which was exactly why he'd come straight here after work to go for a run. When his body was moving, he felt like he was getting somewhere.

The mixture of smells mingled around him: the wet earth, the woodland creatures, the dying leaves scattered on the ground and clinging to the trees. Even the sunlight struggling through the clouds had a smell when it warmed his shoulders, when it sparkled in the shallow puddles.

He breathed deep the rich autumn air, feeling solid and confident, the way he had before he'd ever laid eyes on Thea. He didn't know what he was so worried about.

Smiling to himself, he approached a fork in the trail ahead. The left path led to a riverbank farther on and the right led back toward the shelter houses. The ground was littered with golden leaves, and all the flowers and underbrush had died back for the year.

He'd go to the river. He still had some energy to burn, and it would be cooler near the water.

The wind shifted direction, blowing a refreshing breeze into his face. It was water, mud, wet wood, and…mango lip balm?

He froze, sniffing the air with more purpose. That scent was unmistakable. Had he not been wrapped up in her enough times to know the smell of her hair, the sweat on her skin?

His heartbeat pitter-pattered in an uneven rhythm, forgetting its strong running pace. His limbs trembled with the instinct to rush toward her.

No, I will *show control.*

He continued on down the path, still toward Thea's scent but at a walking pace.

As he stood at the top of the hill, he found her with ease. She was sitting on a bench looking at the river, leaning forward and scuffing her running shoes on the ground absently as she swung her feet.

Her back was to him, and he watched her for a moment. He'd never seen her so at ease, and the image tightened his chest. Was this the normalcy she longed for?

He quirked his mouth. *I'll show her.*

"It's a nice day for it," he said at a normal volume though he was too far away for human ears to hear.

Thea froze, then whipped her head around. Her surprise turned to suspicion. "When you said you'd be there even when I didn't see you, I didn't think you actually meant stalking."

Syver moved toward her at an easy, relaxed pace. "I didn't know you were here," he commented simply. "I just thought it was a nice day for a run. Isn't that why you're here? To enjoy the weather?"

As he reached her, he sat on the other side of the bench from her—fighting his urge to sit against her.

She gave him a sidelong glance. "Sure…"

"How are you doing? Are you handling being on your own all right?"

Thea frowned. "I'm fine."

His stomach hardened. He hadn't been fine. He'd barely eaten and hadn't slept.

"I'm glad you've made so much progress," he said truthfully. "Have you thought about the blót?"

Thea shook her head. "Not yet. We still have three weeks before then."

Syver nodded. "You're right. But it'll be here before we know it." Standing from his seat beside her, he turned away. "Well, I better finish my run. You know how to reach me."

Heading back up the hill to the trail, Syver didn't look behind him. He couldn't. It took everything in him to walk away from her, to not reach out to just brush her hand. If he touched her now, if he saw her looking back at him, the control he was exercising would break. Even another moment in her presence would test him too much.

She was all right for now. He knew she wouldn't lie to him about how she was doing in regard to this.

The congratulations he gave himself internally for showing some restraint was drowned out by the colorful swears he hurled at himself for not staying with her, for not carrying her away to the safety of his own home, for not being the pitiful creature he was and begging her to choose him.

If it was only his pride he had to overcome, he would have tossed it out like broken glass. But no, this wasn't his pride. This was his future, his future with her, and he was playing for keeps.

TWENTY-SEVEN

Thea stared after Syver as he climbed up the hill, an uneasy flutter in her stomach. *What was that?*

She frowned. She couldn't remember him ever being so cold toward her before. Even before their first date, his gaze had always felt intense. But this time, he'd barely looked at her at all.

She didn't like it. Her chest felt heavy and her limbs tense. *Is this how he's going to be around me from now on?*

Her stomach dropped like a stone in a river. Was this what she'd asked for? It couldn't be.

She thought back to every time she'd pushed him away, every time she'd told him she hated him, every time she'd said she couldn't wait to get away from him. The words screamed soundlessly in her mind like she was shouting to the distant stars in the vacuum of space.

The discomfort of that conversation, short and

objectively polite, stuck with her in the following days. Over and over she replayed it. Any time her mind wandered or had a free moment, it would reanalyze the interaction from a new angle.

Over the next four days, she spent every moment she wasn't teleworking deep cleaning every corner of her apartment as if doing so would somehow order her mind.

Later that week, she frowned at herself, shaking her head in disgust as she stood at the trailhead with Eero beside her. Syver hadn't called her all week, nor had he come by her place as far as she could tell.

Have I always been so fickle?

She didn't think it was the case. She'd been with her high school boyfriend for years before they'd broken up. She'd nearly run away and eloped their senior year when he'd told her his family was moving to the west coast. She'd been loyal and devoted, and no other boys could turn her head from him.

She'd been crushed when they'd split, but it wasn't as if she hadn't seen it coming. A year away from each other with that much distance, could even the bonds of first love overcome that many miles and raging teenage hormones? It was a while before she'd dated again.

But even with her friends, had she not been loyal and steadfast? Just because she didn't want to be involved in so much drama, did that make her fickle? Changeable? At the very least, she'd always known exactly what she wanted, and it had always been the same—just as it was now.

Thea glanced over at Eero—chill, easy Eero. He was just what she'd always wanted.

He caught her looking at him and flashed her an affable grin. "It's a nice day for it," he said.

She flinched at his words but nodded.

"I'm excited to see the trail you told me about during our tour of the city. The riverside should be beautiful this time of year. I bet all the leaves are in full color."

The corner of her mouth tugged at her lips, but it felt more like the tug that would unravel a sweater than a sincere smile.

Eero tilted his head. "Are you sure you're not too tired? You mentioned you might be. We could just hang out at home if you're not up for a hike."

Thea shook her head, trying to shake the sticky thoughts from her mind with the motion. "No, I think a walk will do me good, loosen up my limbs a little."

Eero nodded. "All right. Good. Let's go."

As they started up the winding trail toward the river, they fell into silence—enjoying the nature all around them. It was warmer that day, and the sunlight lit the fire-colored leaves of the surrounding trees. Birds sang and chittered excitedly, preparing before their long trips south. Even silent, Eero was nice to be around, peaceful, with no pressure to speak.

Thea could smell a chipmunk a few yards away, the breeze carrying its scent, but her desire to chase it was well in check. She'd been so pleased with how she'd handled her hike earlier that week—until Syver had turned up and scrambled her heart.

Not long into their hike, they began ascending the hill that would lead down to the river, to the last place she'd seen Syver. *It's been five days since I've seen or talked to him.*

Thea couldn't recall ever going that long without at least seeing him at a distance since they'd met.

As they crested the hill, an unfamiliar scent wafted toward them. It was acrid and vaguely reminded Thea of when she'd had her wisdom teeth out. Her nose burned as if she would cry, and a shiver ran from the back of her neck down her spine.

She blinked, leaning her head back as if those few inches would stop the smell from reaching her. As she'd done with the woman in the thrift store, she started to breathe through her mouth.

But her breath wheezed coming in and shuddered going out. She felt dizzy and disoriented, glancing around to try to find the source of the scent.

"Hey," Eero said, grabbing her elbow to get her attention. "Are you all right?"

She continued to search, ignoring his words, but didn't see anything out of the ordinary. There were the same trees, their leaves turning to brilliant yellows, oranges, and reds. The underbrush had all died back for the season.

Thea squinted as her eyes landed on a cluster of drooping purple flowers near where she and Eero stood. She didn't recall them being there before, but who paid attention to every flower while they were running through the woods? She'd been far more concerned about going full wolf on an unsuspecting rabbit.

"I—" She gasped for breath.

Eero searched her face with a worried expression. "What? Did you get stung by a bee? You don't look like you're swelling up."

She backed up. Tripping on a root, she skidded backward down the hill.

"Oh my God!" Eero shouted, running down toward her.

She scrambled to her feet, her palms raw and her shoulder sore. "I think…I'd better…go home," she wheezed.

Eero nodded. "Of course. Can you walk? Do you need me to carry you?"

Thea raised her hand, shaking her head.

With every limp she took toward the car, her knee stinging with pain, she breathed a little easier.

Eero asked for her car keys when they reached the parking lot, and she gladly handed them over. She still felt unsteady.

"Do you want me to take you to the hospital?" he asked, starting the car.

"No!" Thea said louder than she'd wanted. "I have a first-aid kit at home. I'll be fine… I haven't had an asthma attack since I was a kid," she lied. The truth was she'd never had asthma, but it was the first thing she could think of. "I guess I shouldn't have left without my inhaler, huh?" She tried to laugh it off, but her lungs still felt raw, so it came out sad and deflated.

"I guess so. Gods, you scared me to death. You were doing just fine, but then when we got to the top of the hill… I guess climbing hills is the hardest part…"

Thea clenched her jaw, not fully listening to what Eero was saying. *I need Syver.*

TWENTY-EIGHT

Syver paused, his hand clutching the base of a stubborn weed, which grew in the shade of his back deck. He'd heard the phantom sound of his phone vibrating so much over the last five days that he held no hope. But as the second *vrrr* followed the first, he scrambled toward it. *Why did I leave it so far away?*

Rather than rounding the deck and taking the stairs, he vaulted himself over the railing and snatched up the phone before it had the chance to ring again.

"Hello?" he said in a rush, glancing at the screen to see who was calling. His heart leapt at the strokes of Thea's name.

"Syver…"

Her voice was shallow and weak, scared. His throat tightened.

"I need you," she whispered.

"Where are you?" he asked, urgency tensing his muscles.

"My apartment."

"I'll be there in ten minutes."

Without bothering to wash his hands from yard work, without bothering to put on a shirt, Syver sprinted into the house with inhuman speed. Grabbing his keys, he didn't even bother to lock the doors as he raced to his car.

The drive from his house to Thea's apartment normally would've taken at least fifteen minutes if he obeyed the traffic laws. Syver made it there in nine.

Jogging to her door, slowing to a human speed in case anyone was watching, Syver tried the knob first. If she was really in trouble, she would have left it unlocked for him. Finding it fastened, he knocked rapidly as he tried to steady his wild heartbeat.

Thea opened the door and peeked out, then retreated when she saw it was him. He burst into her apartment and locked the door behind him.

Hurrying to where she stood near the couch, he gripped her shoulders and analyzed every inch of her. Her pants were ripped at the knee, and her shirt was dirty. She hugged herself and hunched her shoulders, her eyes wide and frightened. She seemed small and helpless in that moment, and his chest tightened.

"Are you hurt anywhere? Can you tell me what happened?" he asked gently.

She nodded absently but didn't say anything.

"Thea, will you look at me?"

Her wavering gaze locked on his, and her expression steadied.

"Are you hurt?" he asked again.

She showed him her palms, scraped and marred

with dried blood and dirt. "I bruised my shoulder and my knee, too, I think."

"All right. Let's take care of that first. Where's your first-aid kit?"

Following her directions, Syver retrieved her medical supplies from the hall closet, then sat her down in the same kitchen chair where she'd recently treated him.

Dowsing a cotton ball with antiseptic, he knelt before her as she rested her hands in her lap.

"What happened?" he questioned as he began cleaning her cuts.

"I went on a hike with Eero," she started.

Syver clenched his jaw, swallowing the growl that tried to climb up his throat.

"We took the same trail from earlier this week. I was fine until we got to the hill that leads down to the river. And…I don't know what it was exactly. But I started feeling sort of dizzy, and it was hard to breathe. I smelled this bitter, awful smell. I tried to get away from it, and I fell down the hill."

Syver scrunched his eyebrows. "Did you see or hear anything unusual?"

Thea frowned in thought. "I don't think so. I noticed a purple flower that I couldn't remember being there before, but it couldn't be that, right? I mean, why would a flower do that?"

Syver put the soiled cotton ball on the table and pulled out his phone. He typed aconitum noveboracense into the search engine, then showed her the first image that came up. "Did it look like this?"

Thea leaned closer to the screen and nodded. "Yeah, I was sort of disoriented, but I think so."

Syver glowered. *I know it grows in the southwest of the state, but I've never heard of it this far east.*

"What is it? Is it dangerous?"

Syver nodded. "Very. It's called northern monkshood or, more aptly for us, wolfsbane."

Thea's eyes widened. "But you told me it didn't grow around here."

He shook his head. "It doesn't, or at least I thought it didn't. I'm going to have to reach out to some of my contacts. Maybe they know something about this. If not, then I need to let them know to be careful."

Thea clasped her hands together, but he still noticed them shaking. "So…I almost died?"

Covering her hands with his, he brought her fingers to his lips. "The scent alone would likely have just incapacitated you. You would need to ingest it for it to be lethal."

The tension in her shoulders didn't relax, and neither did his. The part that bothered him was that he'd been on that same spot, they both had, only days before. There had been no sign of wolfsbane then, no sign of any flowers, in fact.

He kissed her hands again, and he wasn't sure whether it was to soothe himself or her. "At least you wouldn't have been able to shift with wolfsbane around. Since you were with your…friend, that's a small blessing. What did you tell him?"

Thea quirked her mouth. "He was really startled. I told him I have asthma."

Syver nodded. It was as good an excuse as any. "I'll look into it. For now, let's steer clear of that park."

Thea agreed.

"In any case, your hands should be healed by tomorrow. Take off your shirt, and let me look at your shoulder next."

Her eyes flicked to his, hesitation and uncertainty in her gaze.

"Give me some credit. I'm not going to try anything. Did I force myself on you all those months you were staying with me? I'm here to help."

She pursed her lips in a pout, and he sort of wished he hadn't just promised to behave.

TWENTY-NINE

After drying off from a hot bath, Thea dressed in shorts and a cami.

"I was going to go to the store while you were in the tub," Syver said from the couch when she came into the living room. "But then I remembered I'd forgotten a shirt. I didn't think you'd have one that would fit me, so I ordered groceries to be delivered. I hope you don't mind that I looked through your cupboards."

She told him it was fine.

"I thought steak and baked potatoes would be good for dinner. What do you think?"

"Sounds good." Now that her panic had subsided, she found she was starving.

"The groceries should be here soon. Since you're out of the bath, let's put this cold patch on your shoulder. Come here."

Sitting near him on the couch, Thea turned her back toward him. Then she slipped her spaghetti-strap down one arm, clutching the front of her shirt to her chest so as not to expose her breast.

When Syver ran his fingertips over her bare skin, she shivered at his delicate touch.

"Here?" he asked.

Biting her lip, she nodded.

Ever so gently, he smoothed the cooling patch over her bruised skin. She felt his weight shift on the couch behind her and then the soft brush of his breath on her shoulder. Just above where he'd placed the patch, he pressed a tender kiss—his lips light and delicate. Her body flushed, and her heart fluttered.

"I'm glad you're all right," he murmured.

"Thanks for coming," she whispered, not even hearing her words over the pounding of her heart.

"Do you want one on your knee, too?"

She blinked. *Do I want you to kiss my knee? I want you to kiss every inch of me.*

"The cooling patch. Do you want me to stick it to your knee, or do you just want to use a cold compress?"

She winced and cleared her throat. "I'll use a cold compress."

"All right. Do you want me to get it?"

"No." She pulled up her shirt strap and stood quickly "I'll get it."

Her motions were stiff as she rushed toward the kitchen, and she told herself it was from her injuries.

Calm down. She frowned as she reached into her freezer.

She heard the television turn on in the living

room and the sounds of Syver clicking through the menus.

When she returned to the couch, she saw that he'd pulled up *Scooby-Doo and the Reluctant Werewolf.* She quirked a smile. She'd once told him that Scooby-Doo was her comfort television.

As he started the movie, he glanced over at her and opened his arms. "Come here," he invited.

Without a word, without thinking too much about it, she snuggled in closely, laying her head on his chest. After pulling her favorite throw over them, he rested his hand on her side.

She could hear his heartbeat, slow and steady, and the sound seemed to drive any remnants of her fear away.

It was cozy and lovely and surreal. She never would've believed that such a moment would exist between them.

Thea breathed easily in Syver's arms, knowing no harm would come to her, knowing she was safe and protected.

After a while, a heavy sadness entered her heart. "Is this okay?" she whispered.

She'd pushed him away more times than she could count. And she was fully aware she hadn't given him a proper answer to his declaration of love. She still didn't want what he offered her, and a tendril of guilt squirmed in her guts. Asking him to help her with werewolf stuff was one thing, this was another. How much did it cost him to be close to her like this, to touch her like this? Did he suddenly have more control, or had he already given up on her? Either way, she couldn't help but feel like she was doing something wrong.

"Of course, it is," he said softly, reaching up and stroking her hair. "This is what you need right now."

Thea lifted herself up so she could look him fully in the face.

His green eyes were soft but steady. Was his smile just a little sad, or was she imagining it?

Leaning closer, she kissed him. It was a tender tiny sprout of a thing. It was warm and inviting, lingering sweetly when they parted.

For once, they didn't rush forward, didn't throw themselves headfirst into passion. They let the atmosphere grow and take shape as a beautiful, glittering moment.

Syver reached up and trailed his thumb over her cheekbone, his eyes traveling over her face. Then he guided her head back down to his chest.

Is his heartbeat a little faster, or am I hearing what I want?

She settled against him, absently stroking his chest with her fingertips as the movie played.

Eventually, the delivery person arrived with the groceries—and a shirt for Syver—and he got up to make dinner. Unlike so many times before, Thea helped. She went about preheating the oven and putting the potatoes in while he seasoned the steak.

As she glanced over at him, she smiled and chuckled to herself, thinking he looked too big for her small kitchen.

He looked her way at the sound. "What is it?" he asked, grinning and mimicking her mood.

"I was just struck by this outrageous situation."

"What's that? We have to eat, don't we?"

"Oh, come on, man, you're wearing a floral apron! Don't you think the image of two werewolves cooking dinner in a one-bedroom apartment is funny?"

Syver pouted his lips, looking down at the apron he wore. "I just got this shirt, and the grease from the steak will splatter on it."

Thea laughed, shaking her head. Was this the same man who'd told her he had no control? This was her wild and ravenous werewolf lover? In the light of her kitchen, there was nothing wild about him. He was practically domesticated. Was he so different now from before, or had she never paid proper attention?

THIRTY

Syver tried not to fidget as he sat on the couch. He didn't want to leave, but he really had no right to stay. He'd stayed the night, sleeping on Thea's too-small couch, just to make sure she was all right. He wasn't certain whether his sticking near her was to help ease his nerves or hers—not that it mattered. She'd accepted his suggestion without hesitation.

But now that breakfast was over, he really had no more excuses to be there. And while he wanted to stay close to her for no other reason than to be near her, he didn't want to overstay his welcome.

She'd been receptive to him last night in a way she'd never been before. She'd laughed easily and even kissed him in a way he'd never experienced. Why had he felt so content, so satisfied, with just a kiss? Was it because he knew she wasn't up for anything else while injured?

He heard her turn on the shower in the

bathroom. As soon as she was done, he would leave. She knew where to find him.

A tap at the front door drew his attention, and he stood to answer it.

Syver opened it to find a man with dark blond hair holding a small box in his hand.

Before he could even try to place him, the man's scent hit him—vanilla cappuccino and amber.

The man's blue-green eyes widened to find Syver answering Thea's door. His face reddened, and Syver grinned more as an excuse to show his teeth than to express any joy at the man's discomfort.

Syver rested his forearm against the doorframe, leaning over the man he knew must be Eero. He raised his eyebrows, smirking a yeah-that's-right-I-fucked-her smile. "Can I help you?"

Eero blinked, still off-guard. "Uh, is Thea here?"

Syver tilted his head. "She's getting cleaned up. You must be the new *friend* she was telling me about. Eero, was it?"

Eero shifted his weight from one foot to the other. Clearly, Thea hadn't told him anything about Syver, and that fact made Eero uncomfortable.

"Hey, Syver, could you help me get this patch off my—" Thea called, her voice getting louder as she entered the room.

Her shirt was completely off, but she held the fabric to her chest.

Eero stiffened to see her in such a state—one in which she was clearly comfortable being around Syver.

"Oh! Eero." She flinched, backing up and hiding

herself behind the corner that led to the hallway. "Hold on a sec."

Syver watched Eero's facial expressions, satisfaction humming through him. They went from shocked to embarrassed to depressed, and Syver reveled in each change.

It wasn't more than a few seconds before Thea returned with her shirt completely on, but those few moments were priceless to Syver.

She approached the door, glancing between them. But she would find no animosity in Syver at the moment. He was having too much fun for that. Thea squeezed into the opening beside Syver, who continued to lean nonchalantly, flaunting his superior height.

"What brings you here this morning?" she asked, elbowing Syver to push him farther back into her living room.

He ignored her.

Eero dropped his gaze. "Yeah, sorry. I guess it is sort of early."

"Not at all," Syver quipped. "We've been up for a while, haven't we? We've even already had breakfast."

Thea shot Syver a glare, but he just smiled sweetly back.

Eero cleared his throat. "Right. Um, well, I was looking online yesterday. You said you have asthma. And after your attack and all… Anyway…" He offered her the box, which turned out to be ginger tea. "The internet said ginger is good for asthma."

Thea smiled. "That's really nice of you, Eero. Thanks."

"Yes, Eero, very nice, very *friendly*," Syver echoed.

Eero glowered at him, and Syver smirked. Thea elbowed him harder. He still ignored it.

"Anyway…I just wanted to check in and see how you were doing since you seemed sort of shook up yesterday. I didn't really feel comfortable leaving you, but you kept insisting…"

Yeah, insisting that you leave so she could call me. Syver practically glowed; he was so tickled by this situation.

"I'm doing much better. Thanks."

"Good. I'm glad to hear that," Eero said with a hesitant smile. He glanced at Syver again, and Syver tilted his head at the defiance in his eyes.

"So I was wondering, if you're free next weekend, I know a great recipe for ginger beef. Maybe you could stop by, and I'll cook. We could play a game or watch one of the other Poirot movies…"

Syver stiffened, curling his lip. This dude wasn't taking a hint. He looked at Thea, whose eyes flicked to his. The moment that passed between them seemed to drag out and get heavy.

She smiled. "Sure, I don't see why not. It sounds good."

Eero sighed in relief. "Yeah? Great! I'll text you."

Syver clicked his tongue and resisted the urge to spit the bitter taste out of his mouth.

"Sure. Do that, and thanks for the tea," Thea acknowledged.

As Eero turned to leave, he shot Syver a sly grin.

Syver froze, his muscles tensing to pounce. *This motherfucker…*

But as he moved to step forward, Thea blocked his path with her arm. "Inside," she demanded quietly.

When she'd shut the door, she turned to him with her arms crossed. "What the hell was that?"

Syver clicked his tongue again. "That's what I want to say. Are you still going to see that guy? Why?"

Thea frowned. "Why not? He's nice."

Syver scowled. "Nice," he sneered.

She sighed heavily. Syver didn't want to fight with her. Why did they always end up fighting?

"Don't you think I need to learn how to be close to humans in order to blend in better?"

He stared at her. "Are you seriously telling me you're hanging out with him for training or some shit? Come on, Thea, that guy clearly wants you."

"And so what? Don't I need to be able to control myself better than you did when I'm with someone in that way?"

Syver flinched. "Are you saying you're planning to sleep with him, then?"

"No. Maybe." She pressed her fingers to her temples "I don't know."

A heaviness weighed on Syver's chest. *What else can I possibly do to prove myself to this woman?*

Then the thought, the ugly, inconceivable thought, occurred to him. Maybe he never could. Maybe it didn't matter what he did. Maybe he'd broken any possibility of them being together when he'd accidentally bitten her. Did it matter that she was attracted to him if that wasn't enough for her? Did it matter that he'd shown progress in controlling himself around her if it still wasn't good enough? No matter what he did, he could never be normal. And while he thought that normal wasn't all it was cracked up to be, while he was certain it wasn't really what Thea wanted or needed, maybe he'd been wrong. Maybe that was exactly what she wanted. It didn't matter what Syver did, he could never be like Eero. More importantly, he didn't want to be like Eero.

Syver's stomach lurched, rocking his breakfast like a ship in a violent storm. "Well," he said, breaking the heavy silence. His voice was deep and shook a little. "I guess if it's him you truly want, there's nothing I can really do about it."

Syver's instinct was to just pop over to the neighbor's apartment and casually rip his throat out. But not only would that land Syver in a world full of trouble with the human authorities—not to mention the other mánagarmar—it would earn him no points with Thea either.

Syver straightened his spine. He knew his own worth. If she couldn't see it, if she couldn't see how great they would be together, what else could he do to persuade her? Hadn't he proven himself already?

A deep sadness hollowed out his chest. He didn't want to let go, but he told himself he must.

While Syver made his way to the door, he paused as he passed by Thea. He wanted to tell her that he would wait for her. He wanted to assure her that he would be there if she needed him. He knew the right thing to do—if he had any self-respect—was to tell her goodbye.

He had no words. He simply met her eyes for a moment, then left.

CHAPTER

THIRTY-ONE

A queasy feeling unsettled Thea's stomach as her front door shut with a soft thud.

The expression on Syver's face was nothing like she'd seen from him before. His green eyes seemed sad and lost like an old wine bottle, forgotten and collecting dust in a cellar.

What is wrong with me?

Thea rushed toward the door and out onto the sidewalk, her bare feet cold when they hit the pavement. She couldn't let him leave like this.

Her gaze found his familiar car pulling out of the parking lot. Stepping into the lot, she waved her arms to get his attention. He either didn't notice or didn't stop. She thought about chasing after him. With her newfound speed, she could catch him. But he wouldn't like that. He'd warned her about such things.

I'll call him and apologize.

Going back inside, she returned to the bathroom,

where she'd left her phone when she was about to get into the shower.

I should've just gotten in without removing the cooling patch.

But just as she picked up her phone to call Syver, it started to ring in her hand.

"Hey, Mom, can I call you back?"

"Will you actually call me back? Because you didn't call me this morning like you usually do on the weekends, and you forgot last weekend, too."

Thea sighed. "I'm sorry. I had my hands full this morning."

"What's wrong?"

"Nothing. I was just busy."

"Thea, are you telling me that I don't know my own daughter's voice? I can hear that something is wrong."

Thea's body suddenly felt very heavy, and she sunk to the bathroom floor. "I…I don't know what to do." Her voice was uneven and childish as if she would burst into tears at any moment.

"All right," her mother said in a soothing tone. "Tell me what's going on."

"There's this…guy. I work with him." Even as the words spilled out of her, she tried to choose them carefully. "We went on a few dates a few months ago, and we ended up being intimate."

Her mother gasped. "Oh my God, you aren't pregnant, are you?"

Despite the shock, Thea could still hear the excitement in her mother's voice. She rolled her eyes.

"No, Mom. You know I've been on birth control since I was sixteen."

"Damn," her mom muttered. "Okay. Keep going with your story. You got intimate. Did he ignore you after that or something?"

"No…but he sort of pulled me into something."

"What does that mean?"

Thea grasped at how to explain it without saying it. "He volunteered me for this project at work that I didn't want to be part of."

"The one that's been making you so busy?"

Thea frowned. "Yeah, and I was pretty pissed about it."

"I can understand that."

"Well, that created a lot of distance between us, and I haven't hidden how mad I was about it."

"You've never been good at hiding your anger."

"Right. But even though I was super mad, like so mad that I never want to see him again mad, I'm still attracted to him."

"Okay."

"So in comes this other guy."

"Your new neighbor?"

"Yeah, and we've gone on a few dates. He's really nice, and I'm very comfortable around him."

"But you still like the other guy, your coworker, better?" her mom guessed.

Thea groaned. "I don't want to like him better! He's trouble. He's arrogant and cocksure, not to mention all the grief he's given me. Why do I still want him after all that? It's like I can't stop myself."

"I'm sure that makes you very uncomfortable, being out of control."

"It does! And so I keep pushing him away. But this morning, my neighbor showed up while my coworker was here." Thea clicked her tongue. "And my coworker started doing that stupid male thing where he effectively beats his chest and pisses on my leg"—her mom laughed—"And then my neighbor invited me over next weekend."

"And you said yes?"

Thea nodded. "I mean, why shouldn't I? We're neighbors. He's new to the area, and he's nice. I like him."

"Thea," her mom said sharply in a warning tone.

Thea sighed, leaning back to lie on the floor—her top half in the hallway and her legs in the bathroom.

"So yeah…" Thea said softly. "My coworker was pretty upset. He'd thought we'd come to some understanding, I guess. He did confess his feelings to me last week, and I didn't really give him an answer."

Staring at the ceiling of her hallway, Thea waited for her mother's verdict.

"I don't see what the problem is," her mother said.

"What do you mean?"

"What do *you* think the problem is?"

"I mean…I like them both, and I don't want to hurt either of them."

"But you're hurting them by not making a decision or being clear about your feelings."

"I know," Thea groaned, covering her eyes with her hand.

"Do you really like them both?"

"Yes."

"What do you like about your neighbor?"

"He's easy to be around. He's nice, and we like the same things."

"And are you attracted to him? You said he was cute."

Thea frowned, thinking about the kiss they'd shared in his apartment. "Yeah, I'm attracted to him."

"To the same extent as your coworker?"

Thea snorted. "I've never been attracted to anyone to that extent, *thank God.*"

"So what do you like about him, then?"

"He's…he's exciting. He's reliable. I feel like he would legit murder someone to protect me. But I don't feel like myself when he's around. He's so…over the top, so dramatic. You know how much I hate that."

"Listen to me, Thea. Are you listening?"

"Yes, Mom, I'm listening."

"Love isn't about control. I'm not telling you to go out there and do something crazy. But love puts you in unusual and uncomfortable situations. I know you value consistency and calm, and there's nothing wrong with that. But you had the perfect chance to let your coworker go when you were angry with him. Why do you think you couldn't? If you really wanted this easygoing neighbor, why are you hesitating? When I asked you what you like about your coworker, you didn't say that he was attractive. So that's clearly not his only redeeming quality. As your mother, it sounds to me like he challenges you. And I don't hear that as a bad thing. If you aren't challenged, you'll never grow. I like to hear that someone is nudging you out of your comfort zone. Your head might be telling you that your neighbor is the right choice, but what is your heart telling you? If you listen to your heart and you're wrong, you might make a stupid decision. What will you feel like if you listen to your head and you're wrong? Which mistake can you live with? Which will you not regret?"

Her mother's words seeped into Thea. She was right—of course, she was. If Thea listened to her head and was wrong, she would feel like she'd betrayed her inner most self. She could live with a stupid mistake, but she didn't think she could live with not following her heart.

Still, she would need to handle the situation carefully. Eero was a nice guy, and she didn't want to hurt his feelings. She had the impression he would take it pretty hard.

"Thanks, Mom," Thea said, her turmoil settling a bit.

"So…what are you going to do?"

"I'm going to go to my neighbor's house next weekend like I promised and tell him I just want to be friends."

"And your coworker?"

Thea hesitated. "I think I'll hash it out with him once things are settled with my neighbor."

"All right. Well, I'm glad to hear I could help. Call me and let me know how it goes. Okay?"

"I will. I love you, Mom."

"I love you, too, baby girl."

After hanging up the phone, Thea stared at her

screen. She needed time to think about what she would say to Syver, and she did think it was better to get into it after she'd fully ended things with Eero. But she couldn't leave Syver with the wrong impression.

Pulling up her messages, she sent him a text.

I'm sorry.

THIRTY-TWO

Syver stared at the text Thea had sent him for what seemed like the millionth time. The letters were burned into his mind, and he expected he would see them when he closed his eyes for bed.

What does she mean "I'm sorry"?

With no explanation, those two words could mean any number of things. Was she sorry about their last conversation? About the fact that she'd accepted that asshole Eero's invitation right in front of him? Or was it more final? Was she apologizing because she couldn't accept his feelings? Was that the last time he'd see her?

In his current state of mind, he finally understood why the river of foaming drool dripping from chained Fenrir's maw was called Ván or hope. Only hope, only tense and threatened expectation, could have led him willingly into the jaws of so terrible and painful a fate as this. Hope had led him astray, and now his heart was gripped by the very embodiment of chaos.

He knew he should just ask her what she'd meant by the text, but he couldn't make himself do it. On the one hand, he was bitter that the ambiguity of her apology made it so he couldn't fully let her go. On the other hand, he was grateful for it, relieved. But that relief only made him more disappointed in himself. When had he become so soft and clingy?

Dropping his face in his hands, he groaned. He had other things, objectively more important things, to take care of at the moment, and he needed to get his head on straight to deal with them.

Abandoning his phone at the kitchen table, he took his bowl of what had so recently been absurdly sweet cereal—the box leftover from Thea's stay—to the dishwasher.

When he returned to his phone, he felt a little steadier. He wasn't really ready to talk to Rorik after hearing the man had hidden the prophecy from him most of his life, but that wasn't what was important right now.

Pulling up his number, Syver pressed the call button.

"Hello, Syver. And how are you this fine Monday morning? You're calling quite early."

"I'm calling before work. I'm sorry if I woke you."

"Not at all, but what's so important?"

"I think there's wolfsbane growing in a park near where I live. Thea stumbled upon it while hiking. I didn't go out to see it, of course, but the symptoms she described indicate as much. I showed her a picture of it, and she said she thought it was the same."

Rorik was silent for a heavy moment. "That's… discomforting. We've tried hard to rid the state of the plant. As far as we know, there are only a few counties in the southwest where it still grows wild. Is Thea all right?"

Syver nodded. "She was shaken up more than anything. Apparently, she fell down a hill trying to get away from it. Her hands were scraped up, but they were healed by the next day. Her shoulder and knee should be fine by now."

"By now? Don't you know?"

Syver shifted his weight. "In any case, what should we do about it?"

Thankfully, Rorik let his change in subject pass unmarked. "Avoid it for now. Certainly, keep the newly turned away from it. I'll make some calls. Do you have a P100 mask?"

"No, but I can get one."

"After I talk to those who know more about it, you may need to go out there with the mask and gloves after dark to eradicate it. You're the only mánagarmr in that area, other than Thea, that is. We don't want it to go dormant or spread. It'll be easier to find and pull while it's still flowering."

"All right. I'll get a mask just in case."

Rorik paused for a long while. "Aren't you going to ask about it?"

Syver hesitated. "About what?"

"Eilif called me last week and chewed my ass."

"Oh," Syver said simply. He wasn't prepared for

this conversation. But Rorik had put Eilif in an awkward spot, so he understood why he was mad.

"I'm sorry you had to find out that way. I hope you can see my perspective. A man shouldn't know too much about his own fate."

"Then why even take me to the vǫlva to begin with?"

Rorik sighed. "It's tradition, I suppose. Doesn't every great saga have a fateful prophecy? Still, I was worried about it, which was why I made you wait outside."

Syver couldn't even really be angry. Wasn't he also keeping the prophecy from Thea in case it had something to do with her? He'd rather bear the burden than have her worry about it.

"What else can you tell me about it? Eilif only gave me the words."

"I've thought about it practically every day since I heard it. I've spent countless hours researching what it could mean. That's why I was so vehement about you not turning anyone and about you never making an oath."—Syver flinched—"It's so vague at the end. Why would you be stopped at the corpse gates, barred from Hel's hall? And what does it mean that the Nornir never err? Is that even in question? We know from the eddas and sagas that no creature escapes their fate—not even the gods."

"So you think the child of Hati who is gone and mourned refers to me, then?"

"Who else could it be? It was a prophecy for you."

"Eilif suggested I could only be part of the prophecy. Perhaps I'm only the first part. I turn someone, and I make an oath. Perhaps that child of Hati who's mourned is the person I turn…" Syver's stomach twisted. He couldn't bring himself to speak Thea's name from fear that the Nornir would take notice and carry her away.

Rorik let out a thoughtful sigh through his nose. "I suppose it's possible. I never got that impression."

"Gods willing, it applies to me," Syver said.

Rorik scowled. "Don't say that. Why would you say that? What man would want a child he raised and nurtured to die and be barred from eternal rest? What if you turned into a haugbúi or, worse, a draugr?"

"Better I die and wander in restlessness than she does. I can face that fate with courage."

Rorik's silence was response enough. As Syver's words hung in the air, he realized just how bad he had it.

THIRTY-THREE

Thea took a deep breath and raised her hand to knock on Eero's front door. She'd thought about what she would say all week. It had been a while since she'd broken this kind of news to someone, and it never got easier. She'd never told anyone as nice as Eero that she would rather just be friends.

Perhaps she would've felt steadier if Syver had responded to her text, let her know he'd accepted her apology. What if he was already tired of her nonsense and called it quits?

Her knuckles on the wood echoed the beating of her heart.

"Come in," Eero called from inside.

Twisting the doorknob, Thea entered the apartment. A mixture of strong scents assailed her: ginger, garlic, roasted sesame oil, steaming white rice.

"Hello?" she called out.

"In the kitchen," Eero responded.

Shutting the door behind her, she drifted toward the sound of his voice. When she turned the corner to the kitchen, he glanced over at her with a warm smile.

Her stomach turned. She didn't want to be the cause of smothering that easy smile.

"What are you doing?" she asked softly.

Eero closed the distance between them and took her hand, stroking the back of it with his thumb. Leaning in, he kissed her on the cheek. "You're a bit early. I just put the meat in to marinate for a while. Why don't we watch the movie first, huh? The rice is in the rice cooker, and the meat won't take long to cook up once it's marinated."

She bit her lower lip and pulled her hand from his, but she nodded.

"Oh…" He grinned sheepishly. "I'm sorry about that. I guess I still have sesame oil on my hands."

Thea hadn't noticed, but as he went to the sink to wash his hands, she used her palm to rub the oil he'd accidentally smeared on her into her skin. "It's fine. It's probably moisturizing."

Watching him from the dining room, Thea wondered when the best time to break this to him was. After dinner? After the movie? Now?

At this point, she just wanted to get it over and done with, and it wasn't as if two friends couldn't have dinner together. She tried to put herself in his shoes. When would she want to hear it?

Sitting on the couch, she gnawed at her lower lip. Now. Now was the best time.

Once he sat beside her, his leg pressed up against

hers, he started clicking through the television menus. "What do you want to watch this time?"

Scooting a little away from him, Thea angled her body toward him. "Before we start, can I talk to you for a second?"

Eero's easy expression stiffened, but his voice was calm and unaffected when he said, "Sure, what's up?"

Thea took a deep breath and forced herself to meet his eyes. His blue-green eyes, so calm and pretty, seemed to blur.

At first, she thought there were tears welling in his eyes. But as her head began to feel swollen and heavy, she realized it was her.

Was she so upset about delivering this news that she was making herself sick?

She shook her head to try to clear it. The motion only disoriented her more. Her limbs grew light. She felt as if she were going to float away.

"Hey, are you all right? Your face looks really red," Eero asked, leaning toward her.

With difficulty, as if her hands were no longer attached to her body, she brought her fingers to her face. It felt hot to the touch.

"Your pupils are dilated, too."

Panic seized her, followed by an incomprehensible rage. Somewhere in her mind, she wondered what she was angry about. But that voice was small and easy to ignore.

She took a deep slow breath, attempting to calm herself as Syver had taught her. She knew this. She had a firm handle on her other side. She hadn't seen the slightest hint of a shift since the day she'd hidden in the cleaning closet at work.

Her muscles tensed, and her bones heated. She felt itchy all over—so itchy that she wanted to scratch her skin off.

She shivered, then convulsed.

Thea turned away from Eero, trying to hide her face from him. She had to get out of there. The shift was coming, and no amount of meditative breathing would stop it.

Jumping to her feet, she moved toward the door.

"What's wrong?" Eero asked.

"I don't feel good all of a sudden. I think I need to go home."

He stepped in between her and his front door, blocking her exit. "Is there anything I can do?"

She clenched her jaw as it heated. Were her teeth elongating? Her whole body felt like it was on fire, so she couldn't say if any parts had shifted or if they were only getting ready to.

"Get out of my way," she snapped, her anger and panic overcoming her desire to be kind to this man.

As she was able to form human words, she knew at least her jaw had not shifted yet.

Eero blinked in surprise and stepped aside.

Her hands fumbled at the door, and she prayed to whatever gods were listening that she could get home before she turned.

Racing between their apartments, Thea slammed her front door and collapsed on the floor. Desperate and shaking all over, she reached for her phone and pressed the speed dial to call Syver. Her fingers were breaking, her knuckles snapping with excruciating pain.

"Hello?" Syver answered from the phone that lay beside her on the floor.

Her jaw cracked, and agony ripped through her. She could no longer speak. She huffed out heavy grunts and whined as tears soaked the fur growing from her face.

The phone beeped, and sorrow filled her when she realized that Syver had hung up. Did he hear her struggling? Was he coming to help her?

As frenzy and misery consumed her, she held fast to the fleeting hope that her small apartment could contain a rampaging werewolf.

THIRTY-FOUR

A mixture of emotions swirled within Eero as he stood where Thea had left him.

This was his chance. He'd finally found a werewolf. After all these years, he could perform his blót to Máni. Then the god of the moon, the god who controlled the flow of time, would gain a little ground. By killing one of his children, Hati would be distracted just long enough for Máni to get farther ahead. And that was when he would bless Eero with one timeless moment—one moment in time that he could wish away, that he could change.

Slowly, his steps heavy and mechanical, Eero approached his altar and picked up the picture of his mother. If he wished away the moment he'd asked his mom to pick up some ice cream on her way home from work, then she would've been home early that awful day.

His mother had always been the only one he could rely on. She'd taught him everything she knew about seiðr and witchcraft, despite him being a son rather than a daughter. Generations of his female ancestors had blessed him with magic, and she would have him learn regardless of the taboo, such conventions weren't important in modern times anyway.

It was finally time. He'd been patient as patient could be. He'd prowled the internet for any whisper of werewolf activity, following up every rumor that reached him.

Mrs. White was so worried about rabid wolves that she hadn't even considered a werewolf. And why would she?

It was simple enough to suggest that she break her lease and even simpler to move into her place.

Meeting all the residents of the building had taken time. People were busy. They had work, and their kids had school plays and soccer practices. But he didn't give up hope. Hope was the only thing he had left.

And that was when he finally met the woman next door. Oh, she was beautiful. He even liked her. Somewhere inside him, he'd hoped he was mistaken. Thea seemed genuinely nice, and she liked him. Well, she liked the awkward, unassuming version of him that he showed her.

So what if she'd been gone for a while and returned the day after the full moon? That could've been just a coincidence. If he was going to spill her blood in offering, he had to be absolutely certain she was a werewolf.

It was almost too easy. He felt truly bad about

that. She was so trusting, so confident. She'd told him her favorite path through the park. It wasn't difficult to plant wolfsbane there before their hike.

But then she'd said she had asthma, and he was unsure again.

Henbane was the best way—soaked in a carrier oil and absorbed into the thin skin on the back of her hand. She wouldn't be able to help but shift if she was a werewolf. He'd keep it on the thicker skin of his calloused thumb and wash it off right away so he could wait and watch.

He almost couldn't believe it—almost wanted it not to be true—when she'd started shifting right beside him. Her eyes had blazed amber, her limbs had shaken, and her teeth had started growing out of her mouth.

He'd even had a moment of panic that she might just shift right there and kill him before he could set up the ritual. But she'd acted as expected. She'd run to protect him, to hide her true identity.

He frowned. This was exactly what he wanted. So why wasn't he happier, more excited, that the end was in sight?

He knew the ritual. He knew what to do, and he had all the things he needed, including a mánagarmr. He still had a week and a half before the next full moon. He could see his mom again before Thanksgiving.

Eero clenched his jaw as Thea's smiling face flashed in his mind's eye, her brown eyes soulful yet concealing something he couldn't quite place. He could easily imagine how she felt against him when she'd pulled him into that fierce kiss in his living room. In that moment, he'd never wanted to be more wrong about anything in his whole life. He'd been thoroughly attracted to her; his manhood responding despite everything telling him that she was his target, that he should steel himself for what was to come, keep a healthy distance.

If they'd met any other way, how would things have turned out?

His mom would have liked her even as a werewolf.

He dropped his gaze to the wood and brass staff, his mother's staff, which lay on the altar. It didn't matter whether he genuinely liked Thea. This whole farce was a means to an end. It wasn't as if she truly liked him; she didn't even know him. And even if she did, he still would have given her life for that of his mother's.

Eero reached toward the staff, wanting to feel the reassuring weight in his hand. But he hesitated, pulling back before he touched the familiar wood.

The constant ache that always throbbed in his chest, pulsed a little harder as his mother smiled out of the dark wooden frame at him.

"I'm doing the right thing, right, Mom?" he whispered.

How upset would she be when she found out what he'd done to bring her back? He knew her well enough to know she would never approve of him taking a life in exchange for hers.

He clenched his hands into fists. *No. It doesn't matter. She never has to know.*

He didn't know whether Máni would rewind time to the moment when he'd called his mom for something mundane and stupid, a simple craving for something sweet after a bad day at work, or if time would move on from the moment of the sacrifice with that one thing undone. Would he have to explain missing years from his mother's life, or would it all be as if it had never happened? Would he even remember what he'd done should time rewind?

He had no idea. And he didn't care. He would deal with that when the time came. For now, he just needed to steel his nerves and keep being the easygoing, carefree neighbor Thea expected him to be. He could pretend he hadn't seen anything. She wouldn't suspect him. And why would she? She was a werewolf, and she could easily overpower him if he wasn't a seiðmaðr—if he didn't know how to deal with her kind and didn't have a few magical tools up his sleeve.

THIRTY-FIVE

Syver opened Thea's front door and reached for the light switch. The lamp on the table did not come on as it should have.

His heart thumped, and his hair stood on end. After slipping inside, he shut the door behind him.

"Thea?" he said, his night vision searching the dark living room for any sign of her. He could see the shattered lamp on the floor beside the turned-over couch. *This is why werewolves shouldn't live in apartment buildings. I hope the neighbors didn't hear her.*

Syver froze, listening carefully. The glass door was intact, and the front door had been shut. So she had to be in there somewhere.

There. He spotted her crouched form, glaring at him from the dining room.

"It's all right, Thea." He adopted a soothing tone while he sneaked slowly toward her. "I'm here now.

It's not the full moon, so you can shift back at any time. Just like we talked about before, breathe—"

His instructions were cut short when she lunged at him. He raised his arm, and she sank her teeth into it.

"Ahh!" He silenced his scream by clenching his jaws shut.

She snarled, tugging at his arm as if to pull it off. The fury in her amber eyes was like nothing he'd ever seen in her before, and she'd been furious with him more times than he could count. It was as if she didn't recognize him. Her gaze was sharp, set on tearing him to pieces, but without the intelligence one usually saw in a mánagarmr's eyes.

Syver met Thea's stare and glared back at her. "Let go," he growled.

Even his far more dominating presence did nothing to deter her. With nothing else to do, Syver grabbed her by the throat, squeezing just enough to force her to release his bloody arm.

She hopped backward with a yelp—the sound wringing his heart—but soon began squaring off with him again.

He thought about shifting. It would be much easier to neutralize her if he was in wolf form as well. But he didn't want to do that. He didn't want to hurt her.

Syver moved to the side to place some furniture between them.

"Thea, love, if you can hear me, I'm sorry." Removing his belt, he slipped the end through the buckle to fashion a makeshift leash.

As she lunged at him again, he shifted to the side and slipped the loop over her head.

She thrashed and tried to back out of it, but it was too late. Lifting the leash high on her neck, he twisted the belt just long enough to cut off the blood to her brain.

She went limp, passing out not a second later.

Before she could wake up, and he knew it wouldn't be long, he used the broken lamp's cord to hogtie her legs and his belt to muzzle her.

His hands shook as he went about his work, tears blurring his vision. He hated this. He knew how—of course, he did. Rorik had taught him long ago. But he'd never wanted to do it to Thea. That was what the cage in his basement was for.

This was the first time she'd been so far gone while shifting unexpectedly to need such extreme measures.

Just as he tightened the belt around her snout, she jerked awake. Her eyes blazed brighter and more ferociously than he'd ever seen them. She growled menacingly, and a shiver ran through him. She might not forgive him in the morning. She wiggled and writhed against her bonds.

Sitting on the floor beside her, he pulled her into his arms, holding her tightly against him. The blood from his bite wound smeared into her fur.

He needed to get her out of there. But what was he supposed to do? He couldn't carry a tied-up wolf to his car unnoticed. He didn't have a tranquilizer; it had never been that bad before.

He could only try to soothe her and hope they

didn't cause so much noise that her neighbors would call the police.

Syver glanced over at the television, hoping at least to cover their sounds. It was cracked and lying on its back, clearly damaged beyond use.

Holding her back firmly to his chest, not giving her space to wiggle away, he started to sing the *Scooby-Doo Where Are You!* theme song softly.

His voice was thick and crackled with tears, but he continued on over the lump in his throat. He sang the theme song quietly in her ear, slow and out of tune like a gramophone that needed winding.

How long did she struggle against his grasp? How many times did he sing that song over and over? He didn't know.

But eventually, late into the early morning hours, Thea's muscles seized. Her breathing changed in a familiar way. She groaned and grunted.

He hurried to remove the lamp cord from her legs and the belt from her snout as she started to shift.

After a few minutes of laboring against the pain, she lay naked in his arms.

Her eyes were bleary and unfocused as she stared at him. Her grip on his shirt was weak and ineffectual.

"Syver," she whispered between heaving breaths.

"I'm here, Thea. I'm right here. Don't worry about anything. Okay? Just sleep now, love."

She shivered, and he snatched up the thoroughly ripped blanket she usually kept on the couch. He wrapped it around her as best he could.

"Don't leave me," she murmured.

His heart throbbed. "Of course not. I'm not going anywhere. I'll stay right here with you. So rest. All right?"

The corner of her mouth lifted in the saddest excuse for a smile he'd ever seen. Raising his hand to her face, he brushed the tangled hair back from her forehead.

In that moment, he really felt like the worst humanity had to offer. He'd done this to her even if it was by accident. He should never have gotten close to someone like her. She didn't deserve this. How could he even have the audacity to say he loved her? Nothing he could offer her would ever make up for this.

"Syver," she breathed his name, and it sounded like a sigh of relief.

Closing his eyes against the pain of guilt in his heart, he pressed a kiss to her temple.

THIRTY-SIX

Thea awoke with the warmth of the sun on her face. She squinted against the bright light, opening her eyes to find that the blinds on her sliding glass door were completely off their track.

The gentle, easy breathing of Syver lying beside her on the living room floor drew her attention. She was on her side against him, his arm under her head. His dark hair seemed to shine with streaks of silver in the morning light. Even sleeping, he looked exhausted.

She frowned. *What did I put him through last night?* She'd been so full of rage that she could hardly remember.

Guilt and disappointment squirmed in her guts. She'd thought she was past this, thought she was in control.

She shifted her weight to sit up, but Syver

tightened his arm around her, trapping her against him.

"Just a little longer," he said, his voice still low and gruff with sleep.

She settled back down, returning her head to his arm and her hand to his chest.

"I'm sorry," she whispered.

He peeked at her under his eyelids.

"Thank you for coming to help me. I'm sorry I called you."

He turned his head toward her. "Why are you sorry? Didn't I tell you to call me when you need me?"

She averted her eyes from his gaze, instead concentrating on her fingernail absently scratching his shirt. "You did. But when I texted you earlier this week, you never texted me back. You were so upset when you left. I wasn't sure if you wanted anything to do with me anymore."

"I didn't know why you were apologizing before either."

Thea lifted her eyes to Syver's, a sad little hope only just breaking through her depression at having failed so badly.

"I...I shouldn't have said what I did before you left. It wasn't true. I ran after you, but you were already gone. And then...I wanted to clear things up first before telling you..."

Thea hesitated. This was what she wanted, but she knew once the words were out, they would change things forever.

She swallowed. "I went over to Eero's last night"

—Syver's face darkened—"to tell him that I just want to be friends. But I started to lose control before I could get it out. I must have been upset about hurting his feelings. I was going to come see you today to tell you…well, to tell you…"

Thea could feel Syver's heartbeat racing beneath her fingertips, but it wasn't nearly as fast as hers.

"I love you, too," she whispered.

That confident, arrogant smile spread across Syver's face, but it didn't bother her this time.

Wrapping his arms around her, he lifted her to him. Their lips met in a slow, patient kiss that loosened her limbs in languid desire.

They didn't need to rush anymore, didn't need to take what they could from each other before the other could change their mind.

Heat stirred within Thea, a sweet ache that was one hundred percent human. She shifted her weight so she was fully atop him, the tattered blanket slipping from her naked breasts.

Syver's green eyes sparkled like gemstones in the morning sun as he looked up at her. He reached for her, stroking her cheek. "How are you feeling this morning?"

Truth be told, she had a headache, but it was dull and easily overshadowed by the need he stoked inside her. She grinned. "Like I could go a few rounds. You?"

Sitting up beneath her, he wrapped his arms around her and kissed her deeply—the flick of his tongue on hers sent expectant shivers through her.

But just as he started kissing her throat, a heavy pounding sounded on her front door.

The harsh hammering of reality shocked her into full awareness. Glancing around her trashed apartment, she saw not a single piece of furniture—but for two kitchen chairs—wasn't destroyed. She'd noticed the blinds were off before, but she now saw that one of the hall closet doors was also knocked off its track.

The pounding reverberated through the space again.

Thea looked down at herself. She was fully naked. Frowning, Syver removed his shirt and handed it to her. She saw it was splattered with blood, so she turned it backside front before pulling it on.

"Coming!" she called as she stood up. Syver's shirt came down to mid-thigh on her.

"While I love the color on you, love," Syver said. "You may want to wash my dried blood off your face before opening the door."

Thea rushed to the kitchen sink to clean her face, then dried it on Syver's shirt as she picked her way through the debris of her furniture. She cracked the door open. It was Charlie, the maintenance man.

"Good morning. How can I help you?" She tried to smile.

Charlie frowned, shifting his weight uncomfortably. "I've come to check on your apartment."

Thea blinked. "What for?"

"We had noise complaints on the emergency line,

and this isn't the first time. Do you mind if I come in?"

Thea bit her lip. "Now isn't really a good time."

"You signed a lease contract that states we can enter your apartment at any time we see fit."

Thea winced and opened the door wider.

Charlie's eyes nearly dropped out of his head, and he made a choking sound as he beheld the damage she'd caused. His gaze flicked to Syver, shirtless and intimidating in the space straddling the living room and the dining room.

"Was this a domestic dispute?" he asked, his voice hard but his eyes full of pity when they met Thea's.

She raised her hands and shook her head. "No, absolutely not. Things just"—she fiddled with the hem of Syver's shirt—"got a little out of hand if you know what I mean."

She wasn't sure if Charlie's expression was disgusted at their perversion or impressed. He cleared his throat. "I'm sorry to tell you this, Miss. But my manager has authorized me to serve you with an eviction notice should I think it's warranted. And this"—he gestured toward her once tidy space—"is unacceptable. I'll file the paperwork tomorrow. You'll get an email. But you need to be out of here by week's end."

Thea stifled her groan. It wasn't that she didn't understand. Of course, she did. It was that she didn't need one more thing in her life to go topsy-turvy.

There's no chance I'm getting my security deposit back.

CHAPTER
THIRTY-SEVEN

Syver moved to stand near Thea when the maintenance guy left.

She sighed heavily. "Well, I guess I'm homeless now, too. What's next? Am I going to lose my job?"

He wrapped his arms around her from behind, resting his chin on the top of her head as she leaned back against him. "You're not homeless. I have a cage in my basement with your name on it."

She huffed a sardonic little laugh. "I guess you'll get your way after all." She looked over her shoulder at him. "Can I stay with you for a while?"

He smiled. "You can stay with me forever."

"Well, I suppose you won't have to worry about having space for my things. Most of them are smashed."

"That's a bright side. I'm not a fan of clutter."

She snorted, then sighed. "What am I going to do?"

Squeezing her around the middle, Syver snuggled in closer, lowering his chin to her shoulder. "This is what we're going to do: You're going to go and pack all your clothes and toiletries while I start taking anything that's broken to the dumpster. We're going to fill up both our cars with anything that isn't ruined. And on the way to my house, we're going to stop at Burger King and get you one of those greasy breakfast sandwiches you like so much. If there's too much stuff to fit into our cars, we'll get a U-Haul tomorrow. There's no reason we shouldn't be able to move everything by the end of tomorrow. That's all you need to worry about right now. We can deal with the rest later."

Thea pulled his arms tighter around her. "Can I get extra hash brown nuggets?"

He smiled and kissed the side of her face. "You can get extra hash brown nuggets."

"Okay. Deal. But I want to clean this wound on your arm first."

Syver raised his arm in front of their faces. The bites had long since stopped bleeding, but they hadn't yet scabbed over. She'd really done a number on him, much worse than any time before.

He didn't like the expression she wore as she cleaned and wrapped the wound with a bandage. "It's not your fault," he told her.

She scowled. "Isn't it? If I hadn't been so sure of myself, if I'd been more careful and hadn't gone out into the world before I was ready, this wouldn't have happened."

"Yeah? And if I hadn't turned you, this wouldn't

have happened either. Unless you want to keep passing the blame around, we can only move forward from here."

Thea tied the two ends of the bandage together in a little knot, then met his gaze.

"We're here now, and we'll figure this out together. All right?"

He was glad to see she appeared a little more at ease when she nodded. Standing, she looked him up and down, analyzing him.

Syver smirked. He liked her eyes on him.

"I don't suppose you have a change of clothes in your car?" she asked.

He shook his head.

"Well, you can't go out with this shirt on. It's too stained. Your pants have blood on them too, but I think if we tie one of my flannel shirts around your waist, it'll cover most of it. You aren't likely to meet anyone just going to and from the dumpster anyway."

They went about their respective tasks, Thea packing her clothes first and Syver carrying her things to the dumpster in the corner of the parking lot.

He was just stepping onto the sidewalk for the third time, the top and two legs of the coffee table in his hands, when he smelled that disgusting combination of vanilla cappuccino and amber. Syver shifted his gaze in the direction of Eero's apartment and found the man standing not three feet from him.

Syver curled his lip in distaste.

"A little cold out here to be walking around without a shirt on, don't you think?" Eero answered Syver's clear disdain with a verbal jab.

Syver quirked his mouth. "Maybe for some. But I'm willing to brave a bit of cool wind to give the lady what she wants."

Eero scowled, and Syver smiled. He could do this all day.

Clearly done talking, Eero moved toward Thea's door, but Syver stepped into his path. "Where do you think you're going?"

Eero pursed his lips. "Thea wasn't feeling well when she left my place last night, so I want to see if she's all right."

"She's fine."

"Well, I'd like to see so for myself if you don't mind."

"I do. I do mind, in fact. Thea is no longer your concern."

"Says you," Eero challenged.

"That's right, and I'm the one standing right in front of you at the moment."

"You don't have the right to speak for her or to keep her from me."

Syver raised his eyebrows, amused. This was not the sweet, easygoing Eero Thea knew.

"Do you know why Thea agreed to go over to your house last night? To break things off. You think your nice-guy act worked like a charm, don't you? Sure, she fell for it, all right. She believes all that. And you know what? It still didn't work. She chose me. How do you think this table got broken, huh? Don't tell me you didn't hear the noises she was making last night. I can satisfy her in ways you can't even imagine. I can scratch an itch you don't even know is there. So save yourself some embarrassment, and back the fuck off."

Eero's face blushed crimson, and murder flashed in his eyes. His clenched fists shook with restrained rage.

How cute. Syver smirked. *He thinks he's tough.*

"Tell Thea I stopped by to check on her, will you?" he spat.

Syver beamed. "I will. It was so *nice* of you."

As Eero turned and started walking toward his own apartment, Syver called after him. "And don't worry, buddy. I'll keep this between us. You wouldn't want Thea to find out what you're really like."

Standing in Syver's downstairs bathroom, Thea stared at herself in the mirror. It had been a long day, but they'd moved most of her things. They would need to get a U-Haul tomorrow but only because her bed wouldn't fit in either of their cars.

Thea had already texted Tammy saying she needed the afternoon off the next day because there was something wrong with her apartment, and she needed to move quickly.

But now she was fresh and clean as if last night had never happened. Only her heart bore the weight of her failure. Still, she bolstered her courage. Syver would help her. She had all the time in the world now. She could work from home for the foreseeable future, and she'd save a lot of money not paying rent. She could replenish the savings she'd depleted over the last few months.

She could hear Syver watching television in the

other room. Leaning forward, she fluffed her hair. She wore a periwinkle nightie made of soft stretchy cotton with a ribbon bow at the center of the low bust.

Analyzing her appearance, she blushed and grabbed the short-sleeved button-up pajama top to pull it over her nearly bare shoulders. Then she slipped her feet into her bunny slippers and pulled her hair into a loose front side ponytail.

After turning out the light, she shuffled shyly into the living room, fiddling with the bottom buttonhole of her open top.

Syver's eyes flicked toward her the moment she came in the room. She felt her face get hot as his gaze traveled over her.

"I'm…going to bed. Are you going to join me?" Her voice was a little higher than normal. She had no idea why she was so embarrassed. She'd had sex with him in public and given him rug burns on her living room floor—was sharing a bed so intimate?

His eyes glinted as he stifled a smile, and her heart fluttered at the expression he used to give her at work. Turning off the television, he stood to his full height.

Even from across the room, he seemed to take up too much space. Had he always been so big?

"I'll be up in a second," he said.

Her heart pounded alarmingly hard in her chest, but she nodded once and headed for the stairs.

After turning off the bedroom light, she slipped under the covers, lying on her left side—her back to the door—to make room for him.

She marked his every sound—the water in the

bathroom sink, the flick of the downstairs light switch, the soft creak of the stairs beneath his feet. She held her breath as he drew nearer.

The mattress shifted under his weight, making her fall toward him. Snuggling up behind her, he slipped one arm under her head while wrapping the other around her stomach to pull her more firmly against him.

Her heart raced, and her breath was shallow and uneven. She began to tremble, and she worried what would happen if she shifted in here.

"Shhh," Syver soothed in her ear, his short stubble tickling her neck. "Everything is going to be okay."

She didn't speak but focused on his words as if they were a guiding light. How did he know what she was worried about?

"Do you want me?" he asked, hushed.

"Yes," she breathed.

His already hard cock—naked and pressed against her ass—throbbed to hear her say so. When she curved her back to grind against him, he gave a gratifying hiss in her ear, and she smiled.

"Do you?" she asked.

"Always."

A cozy warmth spread through her. It felt good to be so open about how she was feeling, to share this intimate moment with him.

Maneuvering his arm that she laid her head on, he reached down to cup her breast, teasing her nipple with the tip of his forefinger.

She tensed, gasping as a tingle of pleasure shot through her.

"Does that feel good?" he asked.

She quivered. "Yes." Her voice was breathy.

As he trailed his other hand downward, she felt the warm weight of it through the fabric of her nightie and underwear.

"And this?"

She arched her back, humming a moan by way of answer.

He growled in her ear, the sound stoking something primal within her. Then he froze, and she whimpered in protest. "Thea," he breathed. "I'm trying to stay in control, but you're making it very hard."

A smirk spread across her lips. "Oh? Am I making it *very* hard?"

"I'm being serious. I want us to be together. We need to be able to control when we go wild and when we rein it in."

In that moment, nothing sounded better to Thea than going wild. But she knew he was right. "Okay," she agreed.

"If you can get through this," he murmured. "I'll give you something extra special next time."

She throbbed at his words. She wanted very much to know what he meant.

"What do you love about me?" he asked her, fiddling with her nipple once more.

She tried to think through the hunger that built inside her. "I love that you're reliable."

He slipped his hand under her nightie and into her panties. "What else?"

"Ah!" She shuddered, crying out as he ran his thumb over her clit. "I—I love—"

Her mind fogged, and the heat within her grew fiercer. She was starting to lose herself.

"Focus on me," he demanded, making her quiver in an entirely new way.

She smiled. "I love how exciting you are."

"Do I excite you, Thea?" His voice was thick and gravelly, and he shook against her.

Tentatively, Thea readjusted herself against him, squeezing her thighs on either side of his cock. She felt his jaw clench.

"Yes, you excite me," she said, wiggling against him. He moaned, taking the bait and thrusting his hips a few times. "Do I excite you?"

He paused, seemingly trying to get a hold of himself as he breathed heavily.

Regaining control, he rubbed her again with purposeful motions. "You excite me. You drive me crazy. I'm a madman with you."

His words, his fingers, his insistent thrusts mingled together, pulling her deeper into an oblivion she never wanted to come out of.

"But I fear I'd be worse without you."

She clung to each syllable, the sounds stringing together a meaning that even the pleasure he was giving her body couldn't overcome.

She reveled and writhed, taking and giving elation grounded in the knowledge of simple human love. Her body shook and seized, but it was from the ecstasy of orgasm rather than an oncoming shift.

Moments later, Syver clutched her to him,

shuddering as he spilled the result of his desire onto her thighs.

They'd done it. They'd proven they could be together without ripping each other apart. She glowed with the thought and the aftermath of his touch.

THIRTY-NINE

Syver lay on his side, stroking Thea's hair as she stared up at his bedroom ceiling. It was still early, at least an hour before they had to log in for work, maybe two. He wasn't sure. The sun was up and sparkling in her golden brown hair, making some of the strands appear copper. He felt good, calm, in more control than he'd felt in a while.

"When am I going to be okay?" Thea asked softly, her eyes unfocused on the ceiling above them.

"You're perfect."

Thea's mouth scowled, but her eyes smiled as she glanced over at him. "I'm being serious."

"How are you defining 'okay' for a mánagarmr?"

She frowned in thought, a crease forming between her eyebrows. "That's a good question. What is it like for you compared to how you were before you turned?"

"I don't really remember. I was only a kid."

"Someone turned a *child?* How could they? Was it an accident, too?"

Syver shook his head. "No, I chose it for myself. I suppose I was quite young, but I've never regretted it. Being with Rorik was the only place that ever felt like home, and it wouldn't have been safe for me to stay with him unless I was like him."

"Is he the one who turned you, then?"

Syver nodded. "Yeah." He snorted as he thought about his earliest memory of the man. "He found me on the street if you can believe it. I'd run away from the foster home I'd been placed in."

Syver frowned, concentrating on the morning light playing in Thea's hair. "The people I was staying with… Well, they weren't good people. A whole crowd of kids was staying with them, and most of the money they got from the state went to the husband's drinking habit. His wife wasn't much better. She would smack you well before you heard what you'd done to earn it."

"And your parents?"

Syver shrugged. "No idea. They could be dead. They could be living a life of luxury without the burden of a child."

"So this Rorik, he found you?"

Syver quirked a smile. "Yeah, he found me, cleaned me up, and took me in. Eventually, I discovered what he was. I guess I wanted a home so badly that I would've done anything to stay with him. He turned me. He even adopted me with the help of some well-placed mánagarmar."

"What do you mean 'well-placed'?"

He met her gaze. "I told you we don't really have a structure within our community. We don't have alphas or packs like they do in the movies. But that doesn't mean we don't have connections. We have networks, ways of helping each other. And some of us even work for the government and the courts. Once they knew what I wanted, it wasn't difficult for Rorik to officially adopt me. In any case, I don't remember what it was like to be a regular kid. Rorik would be able to answer your questions better than I can."

"Will I meet him?"

"If you come to the blót next week, you will."

Thea was quiet for a while. "You said that if I make this blót to Hati, I'll have more control, right?"

"It's a little more complicated than that, but you should."

"What do you mean by that?"

Syver pursed his lips, trying to figure out exactly how to describe it. "Ever since I turned you, you've been trying to regain control so you can go back to normal."

"Of course. I liked my life."

Syver shook his head. "But you have to accept that your life will never be what it once was. You'll always have this other side of you that cannot be fully controlled. You have to work with it—give it room to run, to be wild. Then you won't have to fight it so hard."

Thea pouted. "Says the man who nearly mauled me in a broom closet."

Syver's gaze flicked to her face, and he was

relieved to see her smirking. She was teasing him rather than actually upset.

"Yeah, well, there are always exceptions. And you, my dear, are the biggest exception I've ever come across."

Her smile widened into a grin. "Am I really?" She rolled onto her side to face him.

"You are."

"Tell me about that," she urged, resting her fingertips on his chest.

Even that gentle touch, that sultry little light in her eyes, elicited a reaction from him. He placed his hand on her waist and pulled her closer until she was pressed against him.

"I remember the first time I saw you. It was at that fall family picnic."

She smiled. "I remember. You had a gaggle of women all trying to feed you their potluck dishes."

"You were standing in the shade with that blonde friend of yours, and for whatever reason, I couldn't seem to take my eyes off you for more than a few seconds."

He frowned to think of Thea's friend, of the fact that Thea had told her they'd broken up.

Thea stroked his chest gently, and his cock stiffened. "I didn't notice that."

"Why would you? A good predator never wants his prey to know she's being hunted."

She chuckled. "Prey, am I? You seem to be the one who was captured."

"Absolutely," he murmured, lowering his face to kiss her ready lips.

Three seconds of her lips on his, two slow blinks, and one little gasp. His blood heated, and he was ready to go.

Rolling on top of her, he pinned her hands above her head. Her brown eyes shined amber as she grinned up at him. She felt so small beneath him, small but strong.

"You promised me something special," she reminded.

"Oh, don't worry. I'll give it to you if you do one more thing for me."

"What's that?"

He kissed her again until her eyes glazed over and she panted for more. A gratifying need hummed over his skin.

"I want you to tell your little blonde friend that we're together."

Thea blinked, confused. "I would've thought you'd want Eero to know before Wheat."

Syver growled at the sound of the other man's name on her tongue. "Don't talk about him—not while you're with me. Don't even say his name."

Thea smirked, wiggling her hips to grind against him. "Can I tell you a secret?" she whispered, looking him dead in the eyes. "I like it when you're jealous."

Her admission emboldened him, and his cock throbbed and wept with unfulfilled desire. This was Thea like he'd never seen her before. He stared down at her, taking her in. Her breasts heaved in her nightie, her nipples hard and visible through the fabric. Both of her thin wrists easily fit in one of his hands. Her mouth was soft with longing, but her eyes were fierce, challenging him as she always did.

Carefully sharpening one claw on his free hand, he cut through the fabric at the side of her panties. The look she'd given him before she'd headed upstairs the night before had encouraged him to slip into bed in the buff. And his manhood was ready to keep his promises.

Smiling in invitation, Thea spread her legs.

She gasped, her face contorting, when he thrust deep inside her. The sound on her lips combined with the look on her face and her slick heat squeezing his cock nearly broke him.

"I want you to tell everyone you know about me," he urged, pumping his hips hard as he held her in place. The bed protested beneath them, squeaking and slamming against the wall.

"I will," she moaned.

"Tell them there's no space in your life for anyone else."

"Okay." Her voice was breathless as she readily agreed.

He stared into her eyes, fierce and feverish with inner frenzy. "You're mine."

She nodded, her face tight with pleasure.

Stopping, he pulled out of her until the tip of his cock was at her brink.

She whimpered, wiggling her hips to try to insert him herself. He held her wrists fast so she couldn't reach him. "Say it," he murmured.

"I'm yours," she whispered. "I've always been yours."

Grinning, he rewarded her by thrusting deep into her again with a primal grunt.

Her words, spoken in earnest, soothed his wolf into a place of comfort—a place he hadn't been since before they'd met. His other side made no appearance as she howled beneath him, as he drove them both to completion.

CHAPTER

FORTY

Thea looked at her phone as it vibrated again. It was another message from Eero. She frowned. He'd been sending texts all week.

Is everything all right? One of our neighbors said you moved out. Is that true?

Hey, yeah, sorry. Things just sort of happened that way.

Are you okay? You ran out of here so quickly, and I never heard anything…

I'm fine. I'm sorry I snapped at you before. I'm not very nice when I'm feeling sick.

As long as you're okay. Are you
feeling better now?

All better.

I hope I'll still see you even though
we aren't neighbors anymore...

Thea didn't know what to say to his most recent message. The fact was that she thought Eero could be a good friend if he were comfortable being only a friend. She liked how easygoing he was. It was hard to find people like that. She still needed to properly reject him, and she preferred to do that in person if possible.

She glanced over at Syver in the driver's seat.

"Who's that? That fucker what's-his-face?"

Thea frowned. She didn't see Syver and Eero being on good terms anytime soon.

"Well, I didn't exactly give him closure. I sort of just ran out without a word. Then I moved out the next day. I'm sure he'd like an explanation."

Syver scowled as he gripped the steering wheel, glaring at the road ahead. "Write him a letter. I'll deliver it personally."

Thea snorted. "That's mean."

"That's what he gets."

Thea directed her gaze out the window at the fall trees. They'd gotten up early that day. It was a five-hour drive to where Rorik lived, and they needed to get there before moonrise.

She didn't know what to say to Eero, and she

didn't feel up to meeting with him just yet either, especially not with the full moon that night making her feel on edge.

The fact was that she was pretty shaken up about what had happened the last time she'd seen Eero. She'd thought she was getting better. She'd been about ready to go back into the office, too. She'd been practicing with lots of sounds and smells, and she'd even successfully eaten inside a Culver's a few days before the incident; Culver's was always a madhouse at mealtimes.

She was slowly regaining her control again since she'd been at Syver's—likely more from exhaustion at their lecherous antics. But, if she was being honest, she was scared. The only reason she was leaving the house now was because they were going to meet up with other werewolves and for the hope that making this blót would have some sort of profound impact on her.

"So how many others will be at this thing, Winter Nights or whatever?" she asked, changing the topic.

"I'm not sure. It's always different. All I know for certain is that Rorik and Eilif will be there. Winter Nights is usually reserved for family and close friends. You'll get a lot more people at Midwinter and Sigrblót."

Thea was relieved to hear that her first time wouldn't be a large gathering. Since that first full moon, she hadn't spent a full moon outside the cage in Syver's basement. She wasn't sure she would be able to behave herself. If she was going to embarrass herself, she'd prefer if it was around the least amount of people.

"So what's this thing we're going to? What can I expect?"

Syver glanced over at her. "Are you nervous?"

"Yes, I'm nervous! Who wouldn't be?"

Syver adopted a soothing tone. "You'll be fine. Rorik's place is in a sparsely populated area. There won't be other people for miles. Tonight, we'll make a blót to Hati; the first night of our festivals are always dedicated to Hati. Rorik will create the sacred space, probably say a few words, then we'll shift—not that we have much choice on a full moon—and we'll hunt. Then, in the morning, we'll make our offering and feast. Tomorrow night, we'll have an álfablót, and the night after that, we'll do a dísablót. We probably won't shift for those, but you can if you want. Mostly, we'll just make offerings of whatever we killed the first night, and then we eat too much."

Thea didn't feel comfortable with the idea of hunting. She'd been friends with hunters growing up, but she'd never felt the drive to join in. She ate meat, but that fawn she'd killed the first night was the only life she'd ever taken with her own hands. "What's an álfablót and a dísablót?" she asked, hoping to distract herself from the discomfort in her stomach.

"Álfablót is the offering we make to the elves and Freyr—the god who rules them in Alfheim."

Thea blinked, snapping her head in Syver's direction. "Wait, wait, wait! There are *elves*?"

Syver smirked, glancing over at her. "Did you

think we were the only supernatural beings out there?"

Her brow crinkled. "I mean…yeah, I guess."

Syver shook his head. "Not even close. There are light elves, dark elves—which we sort of think of as dwarves—trolls, shapeshifters, and all manner of other beings."

Thea's head spun. Werewolves were one thing; she wouldn't have believed it if she hadn't turned into one herself. But trolls? Dwarves? Jesus…

"You haven't been reading the books I gave you," Syver said.

"That's not true. I read some of them." The truth was she'd barely made a dent.

Syver shook his head, not taking her word for it. "The elves are complex, powerful beings. They can bring fertility or sterility. They can bless or curse. They're also close to the land, the gods, and the ancestors. Let's just say, we want to stay on their good side. So once a year, we honor them and ask that they bless us with a good year."

"And the other one? The dísablót. Who's that for?"

"The dísablót is an offering to our ancestors, particularly our female ancestors. We remember them and ask for their protection and guidance. We honor both our familial spirits but also the female mánagarmar who came before us."

Thea smiled. "I didn't realize the Norse were so woke."

FORTY-ONE

As Syver turned down the road that led to Rorik's, a rush of nostalgia flooded into him. This was where he'd grown up. He'd learned to drive on this road. He'd spent countless hours running in these woods and the national forest that butted up against them.

Never had he brought a woman here, not even as a teen.

They still had a few hours before moonrise. He was glad they'd gotten up before the sun. It would be easier if Thea met everyone before the ritual, before she started feeling the pull of her other side.

As he turned onto Rorik's long driveway, the feeling of home warmed his chest. It was just the same as it had always been—that little house in the forest.

Putting his car in park and twisting the key, Syver glanced over at Thea. She stared at the house in front of them.

"Don't be nervous. They're going to love you," he said, trying to reassure himself more than her.

He didn't think Rorik would judge Thea harshly as the one he'd turned. He knew it wasn't her fault; Syver had said as much. But the man had impressed upon Syver his entire life never to turn anyone, which made Syver hesitant to introduce them for some reason.

She gave him an anxious smile.

After they both climbed out of the car, Syver grabbed Thea's hand, squeezing it while he led them to the front door. The smell of smoked meat was thick in the air, making Syver's mouth water.

Just as Syver was reaching for the knob, he heard Rorik. "We're back here!" he called, his voice coming from around the side of the house.

Syver followed the sound, leading Thea around the house to the backyard. Rorik was sitting in a lawn chair whittling something small, wood shavings scattered at his feet. Eilif sat beside him reading.

When he looked up at them, Rorik grinned and closed his pocketknife before shoving it and the piece he was working on into his pocket as he stood.

Syver dropped Thea's hand and closed the distance between him and his father. As they embraced, Syver felt it had been too long since they'd seen each other. Relief and comfort filled him. Why had he resisted relying on Rorik for the last six months? Well, it didn't matter now. He was home.

Releasing Rorik, Syver turned toward Thea. "Thea, this is Rorik, the man who raised me, and this is Eilif. They've been friends since before I was even born. He's a skáld."

Thea held out her hand. "It's nice to meet you, Rorik."

Rorik's polite expression warmed as he gazed at her. "Glad to have you, Thea. You're most welcome."

Thea's smile was full of relief as Rorik took her hand in both of his.

Whatever apprehension Syver had been feeling about the two of them meeting melted away.

Eilif, having set his book aside, offered his hand to Thea and gave her a hearty handshake. "Glad to meet you," he said.

Thea thanked them both.

"There are some more chairs in the shed if you two would like to join us," Rorik suggested.

Syver went to fetch them.

"So what's a skáld?" she asked Eilif as Syver crossed the backyard.

He we go.

Eilif could have simply said that a skáld was a poet, a scholar, a sort of historian. But of course he opted for a long explanation. He was still explaining when Syver returned with the chairs. Thea nodded patiently.

"How was the drive?" Rorik inquired, interrupting Eilif's long-winded dissertation.

"It was good. The traffic wasn't too bad once we got past Milwaukee," Syver answered, sitting down.

"The fall colors were beautiful," Thea added.

"Would you like anything to drink, Thea? I have soda. Eilif brought some mead he brewed for the feast, but it's best to wait—drunk mánagarmar are even harder to rein in."

"I can only imagine," Thea said. "Sure, I'll have a soda. What about you, Syver?"

"Just water for me. Thanks," Syver responded.

"Why don't you join me in the house? I'll show you Syver's old room," Rorik offered Thea.

Syver stood to follow them, but Rorik waved him away, so he sat back down beside Eilif, wondering what they would talk about when he wasn't around.

He listened hard, tuning into their conversation, but his eavesdropping was interrupted by Eilif.

"I heard about the wolfsbane. Is it all taken care of?"

Syver had gone out into the woods after getting the go-ahead from Rorik, practically wearing a hazmat suit, and decimated every trace of the plant. He hoped it wouldn't return. "I think so."

Syver could feel Eilif's eyes on him as Syver's gaze steadily watched the door Thea had gone through.

"I see you've figured some things out. You don't seem out of control in the way you described."

Syver glanced over at the elder. His red hair had turned white in recent years, but his blue eyes were still sharp.

Syver nodded. Eilif was right. He'd tried to regain balance after Thea had thrown him out of her apartment the night she'd left. But it wasn't until she'd assured him she was his that he'd felt comfortable in his skin again.

"I'm glad to hear it. And how is your protégé settling in to her new life?"

If Eilif would have asked him a month ago, he would've said Thea was doing quite well. And in some ways, she still was. Now that she'd set her anger aside, it would be easier for her to accept. It helped that she trusted and relied on him when she needed to. But ever since the night she'd torn up her apartment, he could sense a fear in her that wasn't there before. He worried that she wouldn't overcome it for a while, that she would draw in and hide from the world. While he was happy to have her all to himself, it wasn't good for her.

"I hope Hati will bless her tonight," Syver said by way of an answer.

Eilif nodded. "Are you going to take her up north to the vǫlva?"

Syver's gut clenched. "Absolutely not," he snapped. While other, more pressing, concerns had been his focus of late, the prophecy Eilif had passed on to Syver still gnawed on the back of his mind. He wouldn't have such an ever-present cloud hanging over Thea.

"Absolutely not, what?" Thea asked as she and Rorik came out of the back door. She crossed the space and handed him a glass of water.

He clenched his jaw, warning Eilif with a glare.

"I was just asking Syver if he was planning to take you to see the vǫlva we know up north," Eilif explained, completely ignoring Syver.

"What's a vǫlva?"

"A vǫlva is a seeress, a prophetess. It's tradition to visit one shortly after you're turned," Rorik clarified.

Thea frowned thoughtfully, tilting her head. "But

that book you gave me said that knowing too much about your own fate would only bring you sorrow. Personally, I don't want to know my future."

Eilif sat up straighter, a grin spreading across his face. "Wise words. You have the makings of a skáld."

Syver sighed in relief. *Thank the gods.*

FORTY-TWO

Thea shifted her weight nervously. She was standing on one side of a makeshift circle, an altar and a fire pit in the center. She wore a simple dress, one she could easily wiggle out of once in wolf form, and her bare feet were cold on the packed earth, despite the crackling fire.

An uneasy tingle ran under her skin, the ominous precursor to what she would feel once the moon rose.

The altar held a wooden statue of a wolf, its dripping jaws closing around a globe that she could only assume was the moon. Empty wooden bowls, stained a rusty brown, crowded the base of the statue.

Syver stood on her left around the circle, too far away to reach, and Eilif was on her right. Before her, Rorik stuffed a stick wrapped in cloth into the blazing fire.

After the torch caught, he started walking around the circle. "With the primordial force of fire, I hallow this space," he proclaimed.

When he reached the place where he'd started, he threw the stick into the fire pit. "Though we may move beyond it, it shall remain."

A shiver ran through Thea as Rorik met her eyes across the flames.

"Hati, father of the mánagarmar, one who is fated to devour the moon, tonight, we honor you. Tonight, a daughter welcomes you into her heart. We ask that you guide her on her path. Tonight, we hunt for you, and we feel no shame. The wolf will be the wolf. As the bear feels no shame for the many salmon he devours, we, too, know our place in nature. Tonight, we run as wolves and live not by human rules."

Thea listened carefully to Rorik's words and to the wisdom they imparted. How many nature documentaries had she seen in her life? Had she ever condemned a pack of wolves for taking down prey? How else would they eat? How would they live? Unlike humans, they didn't kill for pleasure. Their ferocity had purpose.

As the tingling under her skin started to itch, Thea closed her eyes. *Hati, I will not fight you. You are a part of me now. Please, bless me with clarity and the freedom to be who I am.*

Thea clenched her teeth as her bones started to heat. She forced them apart, breathing out against the pain. Her limbs shook, and she doubled over. Her skin flashed with heat. She felt as though she was being torn apart, ripped to pieces and remade.

But she didn't fight it. She didn't push it away. She stared directly at the moon and dared it to run.

Her grunts of pain turned into a howl, which was

joined by the howls of the three mánagarmar near her.

The shift had been quicker this time, still the greatest pain she'd ever known, but shorter in duration.

Thea's heart raced, and her ear twitched. She could hear everything around her. A hawk took flight from an evergreen overhead, the branch swishing when relieved of its weight. She could hear the sound of Syver's padded feet on the dry leaves.

She lifted her snout to the wind and breathed in the forest air. Squirrel and owl, rabbit and deer. She could smell them—the furry and winged creatures that called this place their home. How long it had been since they'd stood on this spot, how long they'd stayed—she knew. She sifted through the scents.

The hearty musk of a buck caught her attention. It was fresh. Her mouth watered, and she raced toward the scent.

Behind her, the three males followed, allowing her to take the lead on her first proper hunt. They stuck close. She could hear their panting breaths.

The forest floor, which had been cold beneath her human feet, felt solid and refreshing under her paws. The sun had just gone down, and she could sense the twilight creatures waking from their slumbers all around her.

She raced through the trees, her lungs expanding, and her limbs moving wholly on instinct.

A thrill she'd never experienced rushed through her veins. It was the vibrant comparison to a roller coaster. It bespoke early memories of her father throwing her into the air, knowing with everything in her that he would always catch her.

Every change before this one had been full of fear and self-loathing—a blur of urges she couldn't control and didn't want to understand. But not now. It didn't matter that Hati would eat the moon. Someone had to do it.

As the scent of the buck grew stronger, Thea slowed, and the others followed suit.

While she had the instincts and abilities of a wolf, she still had the awareness of a human.

She peeked around the side of a bushy yew. She could see the buck, glorious and juicy as it grazed on the long grasses of a forest clearing. It was well past dark now, and the full moon—high in the sky— shined off the animal's dark eyes.

Glancing behind her, she jerked her head at the men. With wolfy grins, they took her meaning, spreading out to surround their prey.

Once they were in place, one of the others let out a howl. The buck, panicked, raced in the opposite direction—her direction.

Never in her life did she think that the taste of hot blood in her mouth would be so gratifying. With her jaws around its throat, and the others at its haunches, the buck never stood a chance.

Her heart pumped in triumph, and with the help of the others, she dragged their kill back to the fire by morning. She couldn't believe how far they'd run without her marking the distance.

As the moon dipped below the horizon and the

sun winked through the trees in the east, Thea shifted back to her human form.

She was covered in blood—as were the others. When the three men approached the statue of Hati beside the now-dead fire, she followed after them.

Thea watched as Syver smeared his bloody hand onto the wood of the statue. "Hail Hati!" he called.

When it was her turn, she approached the idol. Its eyes seemed to glow in the morning light. Dipping her fingers in the blood caked on her face, she stroked the wolf's wooden maw. "Hail Hati," she said.

FORTY-THREE

S yver lay on his side in the small bed of his old room. He was sleepy and content, a warm lull hanging about his head.

Thea's chest was pressed up against his, her arm flung over him. The sunlight filtered through the curtains above their heads. After the blót, they'd eaten their fill of the smoked pork Rorik had made the day before. The mead had flowed freely as did their laughter.

"How are you feeling?" Syver whispered. He hadn't yet gotten the chance to talk to her in private about the ritual and its effect on her.

"Like I ate too much," Thea muttered.

Syver chuckled.

Thea readjusted against him. "This bed is so tiny. How did you ever fit in here even on your own?"

"I haven't always been this big."

Thea grumbled sleepily, and he couldn't quite make out what she was saying.

Despite being stuffed into a too-small bed, they slept well, waking around dusk.

As they shuffled out to the kitchen, Thea yawned.

"Still tired?" Syver asked her.

She shook her head unconvincingly. "These full moons always screw up my sleep schedule."

"Good evening," Eilif greeted as they entered the kitchen. He sat at the table with a cup of coffee and a cold hunk of pork in front of him.

Even after how much he'd eaten the night before, Syver still found himself hungry. "Where's Rorik?"

Eilif jabbed his thumb over his shoulder at the back door. "Outside butchering the buck. He says he's making venison steaks for the feast tonight."

It wasn't long before Rorik came inside, butcher paper-wrapped packages under his arm.

"Need help carrying all that?" Syver asked, standing from the table where they were enjoying leftovers with Eilif.

"Sure. The thing was even bigger than I realized. I'll be sending you home with venison. I don't think my freezer can hold it all."

With everyone's help, they managed to bring all the wrapped meat into the house in no time.

"I thought we were supposed to use it as an offering to the elves and ancestors," Thea said, handing Rorik a bundle from the counter so he could put it in the fridge.

"Oh, we only need the blood for that. I collected more than enough. And any blood we don't use as an offering will be sprinkled around the property for protection."

"You should take some with you, too," Eilif added, meeting Syver's eyes. "You can sprinkle it around your house when you get back."

Syver nodded.

"Will you be conducting the ritual again tonight?" Thea asked Rorik, handing him another package of meat.

"No, I will lead the offerings to the álfar," Eilif stated. He grinned. "They like me better."

Rorik snorted. "So he says."

Syver chuckled at the old argument. Eilif had been insisting that the álfar liked him better for as long as he could remember.

"Have you ever seen an elf?" Thea asked.

Eilif nodded. "Many times. You know, I also had a liaison with a jǫtunn in my youth."

"Bullshit," Rorik barked.

Thea's eyes widened. "You slept with a giant? How?"

Syver was just impressed she knew that jǫtunn was often translated to giant. *I guess she's done some reading after all.*

Eilif adopted his teaching expression, and Syver rolled his eyes. He would have to warn Thea about not asking Eilif questions in the future unless she was prepared to hear everything he knew on any given subject.

"Well, you see, they aren't *really* giants, you know. It's not a great translation. They're human-sized. You can think of them as a race or a clan of sorts. You have the Æsir and the Vanir and the Jǫtnar. They're often at war with each other, but they also marry each other."

"Oh. That makes sense, but still. Don't they live in Jǫtunheimr? How did you meet one?" Thea inquired.

"He didn't," Rorik said.

Eilif sniffed primly through his nose, straightening his spine. "On my honor, I did so. I traveled much in my younger years, and I did many a wild thing."

Rorik rose from kneeling at the open fridge. "Yeah? What was her name?"

Eilif averted his eyes but kept his chin high. "She never gave it."

"So she told you she was a jǫtunn but didn't give you her name?"

"Do you think any álfar will show up tonight?" Thea asked, drawing the two men's attention away from each other and toward her.

Eilif shrugged. "Who's to say? But even if they do, we may not see them."

"Do you need any help setting up for the álfablót?" Syver asked Eilif.

The man turned toward him and thus away from Rorik and Thea.

"If you like," he answered. "We only need to make the fire and bring out the statue of Freyr. The bowls are already out there."

"I'll build the fire," Syver suggested, glancing over at Thea.

She gave him a reassuring smile. "I'll stay with Rorik."

The male tempers cooled as soon as the two were separated.

Syver went outside and filled his arms with wood from the pile alongside the house. Then he took it out to where they'd had their ritual the night before.

The statue of Hati had been removed, likely brought back inside where Rorik kept it, and the bowls that had been empty were now full of the buck's blood.

Eilif joined Syver just as he was using a stick to stuff crumbled newspaper under the logs he'd stacked in the fire pit.

Eilif placed a statue of Freyr—his cock erect with one hand holding a sickle and the other a bunch of wheat with his golden-bristled boar, Gullinbursti, at his side—on the altar.

"Is that one of Rorik's?" Syver questioned.

Eilif smiled at the statue. "Yeah. He's a pain in my ass, but he's one hell of an artist."

Syver grinned as he lit a long match and stuffed it into the newspaper. "Agreed."

As the paper caught fire, the flames spread to the logs, and Syver stood—staring into the light.

"Did you really sleep with a jǫtunn?" he murmured.

Eilif didn't say anything.

Syver glanced over at him to see his blue eyes glinting mischievously in the firelight.

"Who can say?"

FORTY-FOUR

Thea dried the wet plate Rorik handed her with a dishtowel.

"You've known Eilif a long time," she said. "How did you two become friends?"

Rorik stared out the window above the kitchen sink, gazing at Syver and Eilif outside near the fire pit. "We met a long time ago at a Sigrblót gathering. He was the only skáld there—the only one I'd ever come across, in fact—so it was important to meet him. But we didn't become friends until much later." His voice got quieter as he continued, "He, uh, helped me through a difficult time in my life."

Thea could hear the pain in Rorik's voice. She didn't ask him to continue but waited to see if he would.

He handed her another plate without meeting her eyes. "There was a woman… She found out I was a mánagarmr and couldn't handle it. I really thought she would lose her mind. Being a skáld, Eilif knows a lot of people. He pointed me in the direction of someone who could make her forget with seiðr."

Thea's heart squeezed. "Forget what you are?"

Rorik nodded. "Forget what I am, forget that things like us exist, forget she ever met me."

"I'm sorry," Thea murmured. There was really nothing else to say. She could hear the sorrow in his voice despite however many years it had been. He'd clearly loved the woman.

Rorik quirked a sad little smile. "You're very special, Thea—the fact that you could accept this about Syver."

Thea snorted. "Well, it helped that he turned me."

"Even so. If you didn't ask for it, then there was even more for you to forgive and accept. I hope you two appreciate what you have together. Don't take it for granted."

As she stacked the last plate atop its fellows, she nodded.

Rorik sighed out his melancholy. "After that, Eilif just sort of stuck around, helping me pick up the pieces, and he's generally been a pain in my ass ever since."

Thea smiled. "He sounds like a good friend."

"He is." Turning toward her, Rorik cleared his throat. "I have something for you." Then he reached into his pocket and pulled out a wooden disk on a cord, offering it to her.

Thea studied the pendant. It was similar to the statue of Hati from the night before—a carved image of a wolf eating the moon. She met Rorik's eyes. "Did you make this? It's beautiful."

Rorik nodded slightly, a little more awkward than she would've expected from Syver's father. "Welcome to the family," he said.

Thea grinned, then pulled the necklace on over her head and rubbed her thumb on the carving. "Thank you."

"Well, we better get out there before Eilif starts throwing a fit."

Thea followed Rorik through the kitchen and out the back door to where Syver and Eilif waited near the fire.

"Everyone ready?" Eilif asked.

Everyone nodded, and Eilif gestured for them to form a circle as they had the night before.

A hush fell over them, and the snapping of wood in the fire seemed loud as night embraced them.

Just as Rorik had done, Eilif lit the torch and hallowed the space for ritual. Then he turned toward the center of the circle to face them.

A shiver ran over Thea, and her hair stood on end. Her ears pricked as if straining to hear something. She felt alert but grounded, her heart thumping in her chest. Anticipation and excitement hummed through her.

"Tonight, we honor Freyr—lord of Álfheimr, son of Njǫrðr, husband of the jǫtunn Gerðr, god of fertility, peace, and the harvest. We also honor the álfar—often counted among the gods for their power, cleverness, and beauty." Eilif's voice was steady, firm.

Despite him speaking at a normal volume, he commanded Thea's attention.

Eilif approached the altar and took up one of the bowls. After smearing buck's blood—now congealed—onto his fingers, he rubbed them onto the statue of Freyr.

"Freyr, we ask that you bless us with peace and bountiful harvest in the year to come. Oh, mighty son of the Vanir, we make to you this offering and thank you for the gifts you have already given us. Hail Freyr!"

Thea's heart swelled, and she made a desperate wish for such things to come into her life.

Eilif passed the bowl to Syver, who repeated his actions and hailed Freyr in turn. Then Rorik and Thea did the same.

Thea watched Eilif with rapt attention as if trying to memorize his every move and word, trying to imprint them onto her mind.

Lifting another bowl above his head, Eilif said, "To you, shining álfar, we make this offering. May you bless us with health and good luck in the coming year. Hail to the álfar!"

As everyone echoed Eilif's words, a sudden wind stirred the fire, making it roar higher.

Eilif smirked, glancing over at Rorik as if to say, "I told you they like me better."

Thea's heart raced, and she swept her eyes around them—into the darkness where the firelight didn't reach. Were the elves there now? If she looked hard enough, would she catch a glimpse of one?

A light presence, like a trilling from far away,

danced over her skin. She couldn't see it, couldn't hear it, but she felt it with all her being. It was a timeless, magical feeling—much different from the all-too-real harshness of what it meant to be a mánagarmr.

While fantastical and surreal, being a werewolf was brutal, inescapable. What Thea felt now as the fire flickered before her eyes was something else entirely.

It was like winter in all its glory. It was the joy and beauty of the first snowfall with the terrifying promise of the cold it heralded. It was a song, alluring and hypnotic that could turn toward the minor in the next breath.

Whatever was there with them, whatever had answered their call, had all the delight and horror of the unseen world. She wanted to look upon the face of this being, this force, but she also feared what she would find.

"Hail to the álfar," Thea whispered again, keeping her eyes on the leaping flames.

It was enough that they'd answered their call—for she was certain it was them who prowled around in the shadows. With any luck, they would smile upon her. She could use all the blessings she could get.

FORTY-FIVE

The following night, Syver took a deep breath to gird himself. He'd never liked dísablót. It had always held a touch of bitterness for him. His mother, whoever she was, had abandoned him. His grandmother, his aunts, all the women who might yet live and should have cared for and protected him had left him alone and vulnerable to the world's cruelties. Then again, he didn't have much love for his male ancestors either.

But tonight, for the first time, he would ask his dísir for something. That just showed how truly desperate he was about his prophecy. Even this was a long shot, but he could think of nothing else.

As Rorik hallowed the space with fire, Syver centered himself, preparing to open himself to the ancestors who'd never cared for him.

Holding aloft a bowl of stag's blood, Rorik spoke, "Tonight, we honor Freyja Vanadís, lady of Sessrúmnir, goddess of the slain, lady of love and light, you who accept many of the glorious dead into your hall." Rorik smeared the congealed blood onto his carved statue of Freyja, twin braids down her front and two cats at her feet. "Hail Freyja!"

"Hail Freyja!" everyone repeated.

Again, Rorik held the bowl of blood aloft. "Tonight, we honor Hel, lady of Éljúðnir, hostess of the dead, lady who walks in both life and death, you who care for all those who came before us." Rorik then bloodied the statue of Hel—her face half beauteous with life and half gruesome with decay. "Hail Hel!"

The others repeated his sentiment.

Finally, Rorik put down the bowl of blood and raised up a bottle of mead. "Tonight, we honor mothers of our blood and beyond our blood, those who have protected us, guided us, and nurtured us with each step. To the women who have endured and thrived, keepers of the past and caretakers of fate, guardians of the keys and mysteries, we ask for your continued blessings." Approaching the altar, Rorik poured some of the mead into a clean wooden bowl.

Eilif followed suit, muttering words to his ancestors. Syver watched as Thea approached the altar. She made her offering with ease, now comfortable with the process on the third day.

To his surprise, upon returning to her place in the circle, Thea began to shift into wolf form. It went quickly for her, and she didn't whimper in pain as she usually did. *She's settling into this new life. All the more reason, then.*

Squaring his shoulders, Syver approached the altar

and took up the bottle of mead. He closed his eyes and began his plea in a hushed whisper, hoping the wind would carry it to the underworld. "Dísir, mothers of my blood, I honor you this night and ask that you take pity on me. Whatever grace you have for me, please give it now. I know fate may not be changed, nor is it as clear as it initially appears to be. I beg of you. As this prophecy must come true, weave it in such a way that it applies to me and not Thea. I will gladly give up my place in Éljúðnir so her soul might rest in peace."

Even with closed eyes, desperate tears leaked down Syver's cheeks. This was his last hope. Fate could not be changed or deterred. But that didn't mean it couldn't be manipulated. The words of the prophecy would come to pass and be absolutely true. But truth had many interpretations.

As he poured mead into the bowl, a warm undercurrent of breeze ruffled his hair. The tightness in his chest lightened, and his heart warmed. And everything in him said he had been heard. *Then I accept my fate and will meet it with courage.*

After the ritual space was closed, as everyone ate and drank their fill, they told stories of their mothers and grandmothers. Syver didn't have anything to add, but for once, he didn't mind.

After three days of offerings and three days of feasting, Syver and Thea left Rorik's to head home early the next morning.

Syver glanced over at Thea in the passenger's seat. The sun shined in her golden brown hair as a contented smile quirked her mouth. His heart swelled. He'd never seen her look so calm—as beautiful as a still pond lit with sunrise.

"I think I'll head back into the office tomorrow," she said. "I think you were right. Winter Nights, these blóts, had a profound impact on me. The first night was great, but last night… I don't know. I tried to connect with the female mánagarmar who came before me. I thought about all the women along the way. Rorik turned you, and you turned me, but somewhere in that line was a woman who lived with this, who embraced and reveled in it. I just sort of feel like they're looking out for me somehow."

He was glad to see Thea wasn't shying away from the world. She seemed more confident, which made him happy overall. If he was being honest, though, a little part of him was sad he wouldn't have her all to himself anymore.

"It sort of makes me want to call my mom, feeling a connection to the women who came before me and all."

Syver glanced over at her. "Go ahead. We still have a few hours on the road."

Thea grinned. "I think I will, then. Just real quick."

Pulling out her phone, Thea tapped her screen before holding it to her ear.

Syver could hear her mother's voice just as clearly as if she were sitting in the car with them.

"It's about time you called me. I nearly sent out a search party."

"I texted you that I was going out of town for a few days," Thea said.

"Yes, but you also said you were going to catch me up on everything that happened with your neighbor and your coworker. I've been waiting patiently for this gossip for over a week."

A man's voice scoffed on the other end of the phone. "Patiently, my foot."

Thea glanced over at Syver. She clearly wasn't certain whether she wanted to have this conversation within his earshot.

"So what happened?" her mother demanded.

"Well…" Thea trailed off. "I pretty much did what I told you I was going to do."

"You broke it off with your neighbor and told your coworker how you feel?"

Thea frowned. "I didn't get around to telling my neighbor yet. I was going to, but then I…got sick."

"So he still thinks you're interested in him?"

Thea quirked her mouth. "Yeah, I guess. He's been texting me since then, but I really don't want to let him down in a text. I think I should tell him in person."

"That's the right thing to do, especially if you still want to be friends."

Syver clenched his jaw. *Does she want to be friends with him?* He wasn't against the idea of Thea having male friends, but someone who was clearly interested in her… Who knew whether the guy would give up just because she was with him now?

"What about your coworker, though?"

Syver and Thea locked gazes for a moment, and she smiled. "Things are going well."

"Going well? What does that mean? Aren't you going to give me any details?"

"It means it's going well."

Her mother was quiet for a moment. "He's there with you, isn't he?"

Thea blushed, and she turned toward the window. "Yes."

"Okay. I get it. I can wait to hear more later. I'm glad you two figured it out."

"We did. I even went to meet his family this weekend. We're heading back now."

"What? His family got to meet you before we got to meet him? Unacceptable. I'll expect you both for Thanksgiving. No excuses."

Thea laughed, and her mother's faux outrage made Syver smile.

"Don't laugh. I'm serious. You bring your boyfriend home next month, or so help me, I'll be down there the very next day."

"All right. All right. I'll talk to him about it."

Thea's father chimed in from the background. "Yes, threaten them. That's the way to win them over."

"Oh, hush, you. Thea, put me on speakerphone."

Thea hesitated. "Why…?"

"Just do as I say."

Thea frowned but pressed the button. "Okay. You're on speaker."

"Hello? Thea's boyfriend?"

Syver stifled a laugh. "Yes, ma'am, this is Syver."

"I'd like to formally invite you to Thanksgiving at

our house. You aren't planning to go home for the holiday, I hope?"

"No, I wasn't planning on going home."

"Good. Then you'll come to our house?"

Syver grinned, glancing at Thea's mortified expression. "I'd love to. Thank you for the invitation."

"It's all settled, then. I'm going to let you go now since you're driving. Thea, text me when you get home safe."

"I will, Mom," Thea confirmed.

They said their goodbyes, and the phone beeped. Thea frowned down at the screen.

"What's the matter? You don't want to visit your family? If you can handle work, Thanksgiving shouldn't be too bad."

"It's not that." Thea stuffed her phone into her jacket pocket and gnawed on her lip.

"You don't want to tell me?"

"It'll sound silly if I say it out loud."

"I won't laugh."

Her eyes flicked to his, then dropped to her lap. "She kept calling you my boyfriend."

Syver's stomach fluttered uncomfortably. "Is that a problem?"

"Oh, no!" She rushed to reassure him. "It's just… it doesn't seem a strong enough word for what we are… Don't you think?"

Syver grinned. "Oh my, Thea. Did you just propose?" he prodded in a teasing tone.

Thea flushed. "No, I did not."

"And here I was thinking that I must love you more than you love me."

A line formed between her eyebrows. "Why would you think that?"

Syver pouted his lips. "Well, I didn't feel in control around you until you told me with your own mouth that you were mine. But you never asked me to say such a thing."

Thea smiled. "That's because I already knew. You didn't have to say that you're mine. I could tell."

Syver's heart warmed. He reached over and grabbed Thea's hand, then brought it to his lips. "Whatever anyone else calls us, as long as we know what we mean to each other, that's all that really matters."

FORTY-SIX

Thea sighed, unbuckling her seatbelt. It had been a while since she'd gone to the office, but that wasn't what was making her uneasy. She pursed her lips at her phone, which had just chimed with another message from Eero. She had to say something.

> I hope I'll still see you even though we aren't neighbors anymore…

> Are you sure you're all right?

> Yeah, I was just out of town. Sorry for my silence over the last few days.

His response came right away.

Hey! No worries. I'm just glad you're
good. :)

Listen…one of the guys at work told
me about this place I want to check
out. The dunes? I thought I might go
down there after work, maybe have
a fire on the beach before the winter
cold starts settling in. What do you
think? Would you like to join me?
Eight?

Thea glanced over at Syver, who was watching her from the driver's seat with rapt attention.

"Do we have anything planned after work today?" she asked.

Syver squinted in displeasure. "Why…?"

"Because I want to meet Eero"—Syver scowled at the name—"and take care of this. It's bothering me that it's hanging over my head, and I feel bad that he still thinks I'm interested in him."

"Is he asking to meet up?"

Thea nodded. "Yeah, I guess he's having a fire at the dunes."

"How romantic," Syver sneered.

Thea rolled her eyes. "Well, do we have plans or not? I'm sure he won't want to hang out after I say what needs to be said. So we could just stop down there real quick after work. We can catch some dinner on the way, too, if you want."

Syver quirked his mouth but nodded. "Fine. Better to get it over with sooner rather than later, I guess."

Thea smiled at him, then leaned over to peck him on the cheek. She knew how hard this was for him; she would feel the same.

"Hey," he said, meeting her gaze and resting his forehead on hers. "What do you think? Want to meet me in the broom closet in about an hour?"

"You're outrageous." She nudged his chest as if to push him away.

"You love it." He smiled, then kissed her and climbed out of the car.

Thea typed out a quick reply to Eero, telling him she'd meet him around eight at the dunes.

Following after Syver, Thea got out of the car, joining him near the hood.

He took her hand, lacing their fingers together. She glanced over at him, and he grinned.

"You'll keep your word, won't you?" he asked. "You agreed to tell everyone about us."

Smiling, she leaned her head on his shoulder as they started to walk into the building.

No one paid them much mind until after they'd stepped off the elevator onto their floor.

Wheat was standing in the hallway, looking at Mike's phone—no doubt more pictures of his daughter.

"Good morning," Thea said brightly, her hand still in Syver's.

Wheat didn't fail to notice. Her face lit up. "Good morning, you two."

Thea knew from the light in Wheat's blue eyes that she would be interrogated as soon as they were alone.

"Good morning," Syver rumbled.

Mike echoed the greeting, not seeming to notice or care about the fact that Syver and Thea had come in together.

Syver turned toward Thea, giving her a warm smile—a smile that promised a cozy night together. "I'll see you at lunchtime."

Thea nodded, her hand feeling cold as he released it. She watched Syver saunter down the hall toward the advertising office, walking like he owned the whole world.

Wheat was at Thea's side in less than a second as if she'd teleported there, dismissing poor Mike without a word.

"So?" Wheat asked low. "You're a thing now?"

Thea nodded, heading toward their office. "Yes, we're a thing now."

Wheat grinned. "I knew it. I knew you were lying when you said there was nothing between you two anymore. I thought you were really going to bite me when I suggested I might ask him out."

Thea's stomach lurched. She felt stupid now for not being honest with herself in regard to Syver, and she never should've taken it out on Wheat.

"I'm sorry," she told her friend.

Wheat waved away her apology. "Nah. I'd have done the same." She laughed.

As they stepped into their office, Thea promised Wheat she would talk to her later after she'd settled in for the day. The sights and sounds that had overwhelmed Thea, had set her on edge, only weeks before no longer bothered her. It wasn't like it was before she'd been turned; it would never be like that again. But she was able to filter out the important sounds and smells from the ones she could ignore.

As she set her bag down on her desk, she sniffed deeply. Someone had brought kringle in. She could smell the sweet apple pastry all the way in the kitchenette, and she wasn't about to pass it up.

She found only two pieces left when she reached the kitchenette. As she sank her teeth into the soft, sweet Danish, she thought that being a werewolf had its advantages after all. Had she not smelled it from the other room, she would've missed out.

Tammy, of course, was happy to see Thea back in the office and promptly asked her for a list of reports. The holiday season—as well as winter—was fast approaching, and their work was about to get more demanding.

As many people who'd stopped in to chat the last time she'd been in the office, it was at least twice as many now. It seemed that Wheat's mouth was more effective than a radio broadcast. By lunch, everyone in her office knew Syver and she were officially together.

Thea smirked. *Well, that was easier than I thought.*

FORTY-SEVEN

Syver grinned, and it took all his self-control not to cackle like a madman. He could smell Thea approaching, hear her even steps on the thin office carpet.

Christian and Mark were standing at the cube beside his, talking to Rishi about some copy they needed for an ad.

Syver could feel Thea nearing, but he didn't look back at the door. He waited for her to come to him.

"Hey," she said. "Are you ready for lunch?"

The three men nearby stopped to look at her, and Syver spun around in his chair.

It had been unseasonably warm that day, and Thea wore a sun dress—yellow with small white flowers, a ruffle at the neckline—that hugged her in all the right places. To him, she'd always been irresistible. But it did give him a certain level of satisfaction to rub her newfound confidence—and the new clothes she'd gotten that fit her better—into other men's faces. It was a delicious feeling.

"Yeah," Syver answered her question as he stood from his computer chair. "Let's go."

Placing his hand on Thea's hip, they started walking toward the office door, and Syver looked over his shoulder at his colleagues.

Christian and Mark wore sullen and bitter expressions, and their jealousy—their envy—brought him nothing but joy. Syver grinned a malicious little smile at them before turning his full attention to Thea.

"What do you want for lunch?" he asked.

She pursed her perfect lips in thought. "Something quick, I think. I have a lot of work to do."

"Do you want to just go to the cafeteria, then?"

Thea tilted her head. "That's a good idea. Let's do that. I wonder what the special is today."

Syver didn't know either. What he did know was that they—and their solidified relationship—would be a central topic of discussion if they ate together in full view of all their coworkers.

And he was right. By the end of the day, everyone knew he and Thea were together. A sense of deep satisfaction settled into him when they headed toward the parking lot after work.

How many people had asked him about his new status? How many more had whispered about it? He no longer had to worry about rebuffing every woman who approached him in the office. Even better, he no longer had to worry about warding off the men who looked at Thea with interest.

He was riding high until he clicked his seatbelt and remembered that Thea was meeting up with that dick after dinner. His good mood soured. *It's not a problem. After tonight, it will all be over, and we can just live happily together.*

Syver tried to bolster his mood by thinking about tomorrow. Tomorrow, it would all be done. He would wake up with Thea in his arms. They would eat breakfast together. They would go to work together, meeting up at lunchtime. Then they'd go home and settle in for the night.

He could imagine the rest of his life with her. Hours spent contentedly in each other's company—watching movies, eating delicious meals, running through the forest, laughing, joking, making the most of every touch.

He looked forward to meeting her parents, to getting to see that side of her life. He looked forward to their next visit to Rorik—to Midwinter—and to introducing her to the other mánagarmar he knew. They would love her, just as he did, just as Rorik and Eilif had.

Turning toward Thea in the passenger's seat, Syver gazed at her for one timeless moment.

"What do you think about fish fry for dinner?" she asked.

"Nothing like a good Wisconsin fish fry," he replied.

She smiled. "Right?"

They decided to go downtown to a pub on the

lake. The beer-battered fish was greasy in the best possible way, and the potato wedges were well-seasoned. They sat out on the patio of the restaurant, watching the waves of Lake Michigan for a long time.

It wouldn't be long before the winter chill fell over the area. Everyone would soon be bundled in so many layers that they wouldn't be able to see anyone's faces.

But, today, as the sun set, it was still warm—still seventy though the breeze off the lake promised a sharp change was coming.

"Well," Thea said once the sun was fully down, her voice sounding uneven with nervousness to his ears. She fondled the Hati pendant Rorik had made her. "I guess we should probably start heading that way."

He reached across the table and placed his hand over hers. "I know you don't want to hurt his feelings, but it's better to get it done before he gets too attached. I speak from experience. You're not someone who's easy to let go of."

She gave him a soft yet sad smile. "I'll be all right. But, yeah, I'll feel easier when it's over."

After paying their bill, they climbed into Syver's car. As they drove south toward the dunes, they didn't speak. There wasn't much to say. He didn't love the idea that Thea was upset over another man, but all he could do was comfort her when it was over.

Syver pulled off to the side of the road at the sight of an orange metal gate blocking the path that led to the dunes. There was a sign that read:

DO NOT
BLOCK
GATE

ACCESS
RESTRICTED
TO FOOT
TRAVEL ONLY

He couldn't see the state natural area or the lake beyond the cluster of trees.

The moon had yet to rise and wouldn't for a bit yet—not that either of them needed its light to see.

He turned to her in the hushed space. "Do you want me to go with you?"

He didn't like the idea of her going alone. The man didn't seem like the type who would take rejection so badly as to hurt her, but one never could tell.

Thea shook her head. "No, I can go on my own. Just wait here. I shouldn't be too long."

She reached for the door handle, and Syver grabbed the hand that was closest to him. She turned back to face him.

Leaning over, he kissed her on the mouth. "I love you," he murmured.

Thea smiled sweetly at him. "I love you, too."

FORTY-EIGHT

Waving at Syver, who remained in the car, Thea started down the path, dark now that the sun had gone down. Once she was through the cluster of trees, she could no longer see the road.

As the trail widened, she left the woods and entered a grassy area. The native grasses were taller than her, already dry by this time of year. The ground before her became more crop circle and less path—the long grasses pushed over in a twisting trail toward the lake.

The night was alive around her with nighttime creatures. Humanity seemed far away in this natural little haven.

As she made her way over the uneven ground, the sound of Lake Michigan's waves grew louder—more insistent. She could smell the lake before she heard it, and she heard it before she saw it. But eventually, the tall grasses gave way to the tiered sand dunes.

From where she stood on the cliff—not that anyone but someone from the area would call it a cliff; it was much more like a steep sandy hill—she saw the soft glow of Eero's beach fire.

The beach was rocky with broken shells and pebbles dotting the sand in strata. Driftwood had collected in spots here and there.

Eero stood with his back toward her as he faced the waves, the firelight gilding his dark blond hair.

Turning to the left, she picked her way down the hill, making more noise than was necessary to alert him to her presence.

Eero turned toward her, smiling that easygoing smile she found so reassuring.

"Hey," he greeted when she reached him. "Thanks for coming. I wasn't sure you'd be able to make it. It seems like you've got a lot going on right now."

Thea nodded, her smile subdued by the news she was about to deliver.

"I'm sorry I've been sort of silent," she started, staring out at the lake. "I didn't mean to; I just didn't quite know what to say. The truth is…I'm seeing someone else, and it's pretty serious. I could have just texted you, but I thought that would be rude. Is it too much to ask for us to be friends from here on out?"

She forced herself to meet his gaze. She didn't want to see the hurt there, but he deserved her full attention.

His expression was steady, reserved. "That guy who was at your place before?"

Thea dipped her head. "Yeah, I'm really sorry. It's

not that I don't like you… I think you're great. It's just…"

"That you like him more."

Her heart sank. "Yeah, that's about the gist of it."

"I understand," Eero responded evenly.

Thea analyzed his face. His expression was distant, stiff, no longer the easygoing Eero she'd found appealing. But what had she expected?

She didn't want to push for friendship in that moment. She'd already mentioned it, and he hadn't answered the question.

"Well…I guess I should get going. I just wanted to let you know in person."

Thea's stomach lurched as she looked at Eero one last time before turning away to head back up the hill.

She'd taken two steps before he said, "I can't let you do that."

Thea blinked, a line forming between her eyebrows. The waves, not ten feet from them, were loud. Surely, she hadn't heard him right.

"What do you mean?" she asked, turning back to him.

"I can't let you leave," he said simply.

An uneasy feeling bubbled in Thea's gut, and a shiver ran over her skin.

He took a step toward her, and she took a step back. She swallowed with difficulty, her body starting to heat as her other side sensed danger.

"I'm leaving," she insisted, her tone louder and more uneven than she wanted. She turned her back to him again and started walking swiftly away.

"I'm sorry, but you're not."

Thea's ears pricked at the unmistakable sound of a gun being cocked. She froze, then looked back over her shoulder to see Eero aiming a handgun at her.

Her limbs started to shake, and she clenched her fists. This was no time to wolf out. If she could stay in human form, then maybe she could talk him out of it. But if she suddenly turned into a wolf, she would definitely get shot. Of course, unless he had a silver bullet in that gun, it wouldn't kill her. But that didn't mean it wouldn't hurt like a bitch.

Thea raised her hands. "Look, Eero, I don't know what you're trying to do here, but I really think you should let me go." Her words were strained and quiet as she tried to resist the urge to shift.

"It's nothing personal," he commented. Though his tone was flat, his eyes wavered in the firelight. "I just need a werewolf. That's all."

Shock rooted Thea to the spot, her mind spinning as she tried to make sense of his words. He knew she was a werewolf? Had he lured her here to kill her, then? Why? If he knew she was a werewolf, was there a silver bullet in there after all?

Her bones heated, and she bit her cheek hard. With a gun trained on her, she wouldn't have time to shift. Even when she shifted on purpose, it took at least a few minutes for her bones to break and reset. She was still fairly new at this.

"Werewolf? What are you talking about?" Thea sputtered, casting her mind to any way out of this. Maybe she could convince him he was mistaken. After all, he'd never seen her shift, right?

Eero snorted distastefully. "Come on, Thea. Do you really think I didn't do my research? Do you think I would just point a gun at an innocent woman without proof?"

"Quite honestly, I don't know what to believe," Thea said. "It seems I completely misjudged you. I certainly never thought you'd pull a gun on me."

Eero frowned. "I'm sorry about this. I really do like you, Thea, even if you are a werewolf. I wish things could've been different."

Thea didn't like the hopeless finality she heard in his voice. "You don't have to do this, Eero."

He shook his head. "No, I do. And don't even try to shift. I've already cast a spell on this area that makes it impossible for you to do so."

Fear crawled up Thea's legs and into her spine. If she couldn't shift at all, she only had the defenses of an average woman. She stiffened, that thought triggering something in her mind.

"A spell?" she asked, slowly lowering her hands and slipping one into her bag, which was strapped across her body and open at her hip. "What? Do you think you're some kind of wizard?"

Eero squinted at her, clearly displeased. "You've never heard of seiðr? What kind of mánagarmr are you?"

Thea recognized the word from something Rorik had mentioned. "I don't know what any of that is." She slipped her thumb under the flip top of the pepper spray her parents had gotten her.

Pulling it from her bag, she pressed down, aiming the stream at Eero.

The wind carried most of it away from them, but as he hissed and cried out in pain, she used the opportunity to scramble up the path.

FORTY-NINE

Eero's eyes burned, tears streaming down his face as he tried to clear his vision. His chest was tight, and his heart screamed in panic and desperation.

He'd hesitated when he'd seen the fear in Thea's eyes. He shouldn't have let her get that far. He should have shot her in the back. He was losing his chance. She was getting away.

Eero squinted against his bleary vision and the darkness outside the firelight. He could just make out Thea's yellow dress, fluttering in the breeze as she scrambled up the path. He could hear her breath, uneven with fear.

Pushing through the burning pain, he took aim.

A growl, primal and bone-chilling, came from his right. He swung around just in time to see a wolf leaping off the top of the hill toward him. Its limbs were long and taut, and its eyes were locked on him.

Its sharp teeth were bared and ready to tear into his flesh.

Eero's finger squeezed the trigger, sending his silver bullet to its deadly purpose. The wolf fell like a rock, skidding down the dune in a flurry of sand.

Eero's ears rang from the crack of the gun. Passing his hand over his eyes, he spoke a spell his mother had taught him long ago while they'd volunteered at the sight center—one to ease pain and clear vision.

As the fog lifted from his eyes, he saw Thea scrambling toward the man at the bottom of the hill. He must have entered the boundary of Eero's spell because he was no longer in wolf form.

The ringing in Eero's ears eased only to be replaced by Thea's wails.

She sat on the ground, cradling the man's head as blood seeped from his chest.

"No, Syver, look at me!" she screamed.

But the silver bullet had done its work. Syver was no more.

Eero felt cold, numb. Somewhere in the back of his mind, he confirmed his suspicions about Thea's friend. After he'd seen the bandage on the man's forearm the night following Eero dosing her with henbane, he knew Syver was either a werewolf himself, or, at the very least, Syver knew Thea was one.

This worked out better for him. He got his werewolf, and he hadn't had to kill Thea. He really hadn't wanted to kill Thea.

But as he stood there, her sobs louder than the

crashing waves of Lake Michigan, he couldn't make himself feel anything.

This numbness was foreign to him, he'd always felt everything so keenly—his joys, his sorrows, his unbearable grief.

Grief was what Thea was feeling now—the same grief he'd felt for the last few years. He knew that, but he didn't sympathize. He couldn't.

A jolt of fear shot through him—that he felt quite clearly. He'd lost something, something precious to him, something his mother had always praised him for.

When she returned to him, would he get it back? Was it gone forever? His chest tightened, and he couldn't take a full breath.

The moonlight, rising over the lake, struck him like a high beam, and the world around him stilled.

He could no longer hear Thea's cries of despair; he couldn't hear the sound of the waves. He glanced around. Everything was frozen in timelessness—the rippling water, the flames of his fire, even Thea's breathing.

A voice, ethereal and distant, whispered into his ear, and Eero knew it was the voice of Máni, god of the moon. "A moment for a moment, a life for a life—what would you change?"

Eero trembled. His knees buckled, and he dropped to the sand. His mind whirled. He couldn't believe it had worked. For the price of one arrogant werewolf, he could have his mother back. He could undo one silly mistake that had cost him everything.

He glanced over his shoulder at Thea, her face

frozen in unrestrained agony. For a long moment, he couldn't look away. This image of her was sharply—brutally—fascinating in a raw humanity kind of way. She perfectly captured the worst feeling imaginable—a feeling brought on by the worst humanity had to offer.

Eero closed his eyes, tears trailing down his face. Whispering his wish to the moon, a new pain weighed down his heart.

Eero took a shallow broken breath. And when he opened his eyes, the world yet again moved around him.

"I understand," Eero found himself saying, standing where he had just knelt.

Thea's brown eyes, glinting amber in the firelight, analyzed him. He tried to mask his expression as tears welled in his eyes. He tried to swallow but found that he'd forgotten how.

Thea bit her lip, her sympathy clear in her gaze. But she would never know that it was not her rejection that made him cry in this moment.

She hesitated, gripping the strap of her bag with two hands. "Well…I guess I should get going. I just wanted to let you know in person."

Eero dipped his head in a nod. He had no words to give her. Releasing the cold metal of the gun in his jacket pocket, Eero turned toward the lake and the gentle moonlight that shined off the waves.

Without another word, Thea turned toward the path that led up the hill and slowly started walking back—back to Syver and back to her life.

Eero didn't watch her go. He kept his eyes trained on the moon.

All the emotions that had gone cold were firmly back in place—gnawing at Eero's heart. But he breathed easy for they were far lighter to carry than their absence had been to bear.

"Hail Máni," Eero whispered, his voice unheard over the crashing waves. But, to him, the moonlight seemed to shine just a bit brighter.

FIFTY

Syver shifted his weight from one foot to the other. He hadn't felt this nervous in weeks—not since that night he'd followed Thea through the trees and brush to the dunes. Since then, he'd had the inexplicable feeling that everything would be all right.

But now, his heart pounded, and his palms were sweaty as he stood on the front porch this cold November morning.

Thea smiled up at him, but that only made him more nervous somehow.

After a few more heavy breaths, the door before them opened. A tall woman with eyes the color of Thea's and hair a few shades darker—and much shorter—grinned at them through round glasses.

"Happy Thanksgiving!" she squealed, pulling Thea off the doorstep and into her embrace. "I'm so glad you're here! I missed you so much, baby girl!"

Thea's mom hugged her for a long time.

Thea chuckled. "Mom, you're choking me."

Her mom released her, but she didn't look pleased about it. Her eyes shifted to Syver, and he stood up straighter.

Was his smile too big? Was he showing too many teeth?

"You must be Syver," she said, breaking into a wide grin. "Come here. We're a hugging family."

Thea's mom opened her arms to him, her expression warm and welcoming.

Though she was a tall woman, she was quite thin, and Syver felt he needed to be gentle as he embraced her. She patted him softly on the back, the comforting gesture putting him at ease.

"Come in," she urged them. "Your dad is in the den watching the game. Everyone won't be here for a while, so relax while you can. Once Sharon and the kids get here, it'll be chaos as usual."

Thea had warned Syver about her Aunt Sharon's grandchildren. Apparently, they were a rambunctious brood.

As Thea's mom led them through the living room and into the kitchen, Syver memorized every inch of the place. This was where Thea had grown up. How many secrets did it hold?

Once they reached the kitchen, Thea's mom tilted her head toward a room beyond—where a man sat watching the Lions-Bears game on the television.

Syver followed Thea into the den.

Coming up behind him, Thea wrapped her arms around her dad's neck, kissing him on the head. "Happy Thanksgiving, Dad," she said.

Her dad stood to embrace her. "Happy Thanksgiving."

His gaze met Syver's, and Syver froze. He'd never met the father of anyone he'd dated—it had never been this serious.

He bowed his head at the man and offered his hand. "It's nice to meet you, sir. I'm Syver."

Thea's dad stared at him hard, folding his arms. Syver hesitated, his hand hanging out there in thin air.

Scowling, Thea smacked her dad on the shoulder. "Stop."

Her dad broke into a grin and clasped Syver's hand firmly. "I'm just kidding. Have a seat. Do you like football? Can I get you a beer?"

Syver had never paid sports much attention. It wasn't as if he could play without hurting someone. But he was happy to sit in communal silence with her father and watch something he enjoyed.

Thea's mother called for Thea in the kitchen.

Syver hesitated.

"Go ahead and sit here with Dad. Mom is particular about who she lets help her in the kitchen," Thea said, giving his hand a squeeze.

Syver sat down on the couch and faced the television as an awkward silence settled between the two men. What was the etiquette for watching football with someone you'd just met? Did he talk? Did he remain silent so as not to interrupt?

"Yeah, she's been like that since the rock brownie incident," Thea's dad commented.

Syver tilted his head. "The rock brownie incident?"

Thea's dad smirked. "Yeah, she was making brownies one time, and she nearly burned the house down."

"That wasn't my fault!" Thea's mother called from the kitchen. "Thea was still young, and she turned the temperature knob on the oven up without me knowing."

Syver blinked. How had she even heard what her husband had said all the way in the kitchen? Did she have supernatural hearing, too?

"Sure, sure, blame it on the baby," Thea's dad teased his wife, grinning.

Her mom came out from the kitchen and offered Syver a beer, which he took with thanks. He wasn't sure if she heard him though because her annoyed expression was aimed at her husband.

"You keep this up, and you'll get no dessert," she snapped.

"I haven't had dessert in years from fear that my teeth would fall out of my head," he muttered.

Syver's eyes shifted between them. He wasn't sure if he was supposed to laugh or not. Was this normal for them?

Thea's mother removed a soft, fluffy slipper from her foot and aimed it right at her husband, hitting him on the side of the head.

He caught it as it bounced off him and hugged it to his chest.

"Give me my slipper," she demanded, standing on one foot.

"It's my slipper now," he said.

"It wouldn't even fit your big-ass feet."

Removing his own house shoe, Thea's dad stuffed his foot into his wife's slipper. Then he stood, walking slowly toward her.

Her eyes widened. "What are you doing?"

"Getting the other one," he said. "I want to match."

Her mom squealed, turning to run. But her husband caught her around the waist and threw her over his shoulder.

She laughed and screamed as he peeled the shoe off her kicking foot.

Placing her back on her now bare feet, he put on the other slipper.

It was something to see, a grown man standing there in his wife's fluffy kitty slippers, wearing a serious expression of triumph.

Syver bit his cheek, trying hard not to laugh.

"You two are ridiculous," Thea remarked from the doorway to the kitchen. "I'll be lucky if Syver ever wants to see me again after this."

Her mother laughed, smiling over at Syver. "Oh, it's already too late. He can't escape us now. We're keeping him."

Turning his attention toward Thea, Syver grinned the smile he knew she couldn't resist. "You couldn't get rid of me if you tried."

AFTERWORD

Thank you for reading! I do so hope you enjoyed it. If you have a moment, I would very much appreciate a review on the store where you bought it. Tell other readers what you thought, and help them make a decision on this book.

If you'd like to stay updated on news about my books and events, you can subscribe to my newsletter on my website: www.dlieber.com

Thanks again! I hope you will travel through my worlds with me again in the future.

D. Lieber

ABOUT THE AUTHOR

D. Lieber has a wanderlust that would make a butterfly envious. When she isn't planning her next physical adventure, she's recklessly jumping from one fictional world to another. Her love of reading led her to earn a Bachelor's in English from Wright State University.

Beyond her skeptic and slightly pessimistic mind, Lieber wants to believe. She has been many places—from Canada to England, France to Italy, Germany to Russia—believing that a better world comes from putting a face on "other." She is a romantic idealist at heart, always fighting to keep her feet on the ground and her head in the clouds.

Lieber lives in Wisconsin with her husband (John) and cats (Yin and Nox).

LINKS

Website: dlieber.com
Goodreads: goodreads.com/dlieberwriting
Bookbub: bookbub.com/profile/d-lieber